Fearless

BOULEVARD *of* DREAMS

MANDY GONZALEZ

with BRITTANY J. THURMAN

ALADDIN

New York   London   Toronto   Sydney   New Delhi

Our mothers, Robin and Tia,
and our grandmothers, Grandma Marie and Gran-Gran.
Without you, there would be no words

ALADDIN

An imprint of Simon & Schuster Children's Publishing Division

1230 Avenue of the Americas, New York, New York 10020

First Aladdin hardcover edition April 2022

Text copyright © 2022 by In This Together Media, LLC; and Mandy Gonzalez

Jacket illustrations copyright © 2022 by Geraldine Rodriguez

All rights reserved, including the right of reproduction in whole or in part in any form.

ALADDIN and related logo are registered trademarks of Simon & Schuster, Inc.

For information about special discounts for bulk purchases, please contact Simon & Schuster Special Sales at 1-866-506-1949 or business@simonandschuster.com.

The Simon & Schuster Speakers Bureau can bring authors to your live event. For more information or to book an event contact the Simon & Schuster Speakers Bureau at 1-866-248-3049 or visit our website at www.simonspeakers.com.

Designed by Laura Lyn DiSiena

The text of this book was set in Bookman Old Style.

Manufactured in the United States of America 0222 FFG

10 9 8 7 6 5 4 3 2 1

Library of Congress Control Number 2021940134

ISBN 978-1-5344-6898-6 (hc)

ISBN 978-1-5344-6900-6 (ebook)

One

THE MAN ON THE STAGE
Tuesday

Relly L. Morton could dance where there was no stage. Everybody from grandmommas braiding hair on front stoops to the incense man trying to make a sale took note. Harlem knew Relly as the kid who danced from Marcus Garvey Park to the barbershop. From the Schomburg Center to the Apollo. If Relly L. Morton was not dancing, the world may as well quit spinning.

"Broadway!" a man selling Harlem T-shirts shouted, giving Relly a nod.

"You the boss round here!"

"Boss" was Relly's nickname.

It was a bright blue Monday in March when Relly used

the rail of a nearby brownstone to pretend it was a barre. He needed to warm up each muscle before the evening show. Sure, all the actors could warm up at the Ethel Merman Theater, but why wait until he got there? As he grabbed the rail, he bent his knees. He moved slow, stretching down, then lifting himself back up. *Slower.* Down, then back up. *Steady.* Down, up. Three quick pliés as his brother, Bobby, crossed the street.

"Really, Relly? In the middle of Seventh Avenue!"

The brothers were on their way to 132nd Street. Relly nodded back to the T-shirt man as he eased into a walking dance, a dancing walk. Then he hopped the curb, lifting his feet off the ground until they were on their points. Tiptoes. Relly did a quick triple-time step, thinking of the move he would do on stage during the show's opening number.

The role of Pax in the Broadway musical *Our Time* called for Relly to be flexible, nimble, alert. Each show was a performance, each performance broken into acts. Each act was a workout. The show opened back in November. Since then, *Our Time* had sold out every day by noon. When tickets opened, they were gone in minutes. Even though it had only been four months since the start of the hit show, Relly felt he had been on Broadway for a lifetime.

This was on his mind as Relly ignored his brother, concentrating on loosening his muscles. At the corner, he did a brush tap that made his foot go forward. It hovered over the smashed gum on the sidewalk. Crossing 129th Street, Relly's feet did a single Cincinnati time step. He dug his heels into the sidewalk, then shuffled and brought them back. The move was in tune with the chime of the pedestrian walk sign.

When Relly walked, he danced. When Relly danced, he tapped. And Relly's taps had zeal. Even if he had on sneakers, Relly's dancing had essence.

"Hurry up, Relly!"

"I'm trying!"

Relly let both feet riff. Three counts, three beats against the sidewalk as he stepped past a toddler sound asleep in her stroller. Then he swiveled and swirled into the grand finale, an array of toe stands and rubber legs. Left and right, front and back, zigzag moves that made him feel free as a golden eagle taking off in flight. The motion of Relly's feet was a force on the ground. A force so strong, it lifted him straight into Juanita's door.

In the middle of Harlem, Juanita's Market was known for cheese sandwiches and a cat named Harold, and the cheapest pineapples this side of the Hudson.

"What surprise come through my door this evening? Mr. Morton himself!" said the woman behind the deli counter, Juanita.

"Harlem's Broadway star. You come to let me have your autograph? You come to teach me some of your moves?" she joked, lifting her left foot forward and backward, showing off her own moves. Her off-white apron had the green embroidered nickname "Nita."

Relly inhaled the scent of beef and toasted bread. Melted cheese and freshly cut tomatoes. Then, the smell of cleaning solution. His feet were still in movement doing quick tap moves across the bodega floor. In front of the candy stand, Relly was on his toes, then back down with his heels to the floor. Toes again, then heels to the floor. Up, down. Up, down.

"Nah, not today. We've come to get some groceries, Nita," said Bobby, picking up a silver basket. Relly's moves must have been a little too swift, because Bobby gripped Relly by the shoulders and squeezed so tight, Relly felt his soul leave his body. A yelp left his mouth.

"Ow!"

Bobby twisted his brother around.

"I'm begging you. Swear I'll give you the most valuable thing I own if you teach yourself how to be still."

"Valuable?" Relly asked, pausing to take a step back from his brother's grip. It wasn't that Bobby didn't have valuable possessions, but Relly was trying to think of a comeback. "You mean like those socks you collect? I'll pass." The two brothers were used to exchanging words back and forth. Relly, being the brother who could not keep still, naturally annoyed his older brother Bobby. Bobby was quiet and calm. Bobby hated excess noise and could always be found with a textbook on his lap.

"Be studious, Relly. Open a book like your brother instead of doing all that running and jumping, commotion-making round the living room," their grandfather said before the brothers left the house. Bickering or not, aggravation or nah, it was all love.

"Ha!" came Nita's laugh from behind the counter. She wiped her hands on a cloth as Relly slid farther from Bobby's reach.

"I'm serious, Relly."

"You? Serious? You better catch me first." Relly did a quick turn, a fouetté in the middle of the floor, almost knocking over the rows of Kit Kats and Twizzlers with his stretched-out leg. He stood back on his two feet, easing away from the stand.

"Listen to your brother, Relly," said Nita. "Love you both, but you knock over even one shelf, it'll be you behind this counter making cheese sandwiches. That's a promise."

Relly couldn't tell if Nita was serious or playing. He was not about to take a chance and find out. Before they stopped in the store, the sun had already started to tire. Its bright yellow hue had been exchanged for a muted orange. The last thing Relly needed was to be late for sign-in on account of destroying Nita's store.

"Noted!" Relly caught his reflection in the bodega window. Then he caught Bobby's side-eye and narrowed eyebrows. The pointed look that told Relly to apologize.

"I mean, I hear you, Nita! Sorry. Will not happen again. Promise!"

The afternoon sun gave Relly's deep brown skin a glow. Same shade as his momma's, a shade darker than Bobby's, a match to his grandfather Gregory's complexion. Relly smiled, pleased with the dye job he had done on his hair. A purple mixed with pink that reminded Relly of a Jean-Michel Basquiat painting. He forgot the title, but he never forgot the colors during that third-grade school field trip to a SoHo art gallery. Only thing different about Relly was his height, if anybody dared call five foot three short for a twelve-year-old.

"You got the list?" Relly caught up with Bobby down the baked-goods aisle. "Dang, you're fast." That quick, the basket in Bobby's hand was stuffed with sugar, salt, plus a giant bag of pecans. Bobby handed Relly the creased piece of paper and nodded toward the aisle of canned goods. Relly hadn't been able to figure out why Momma wanted to make a pineapple upside-down cake for his and Bobby's grandfather's birthday. Thursday was almost a whole three days away. Plenty of time to buy a real cake. One full of buttercream.

"Get the rest," Bobby instructed.

"You literally almost got it all."

"Imma ask Nita to make me a sandwich."

There were only two items left on the list to pick up. Pineapples and cherries. The two most important pineapple upside-down cake ingredients. Relly walked down the aisle, passing up the artichokes, green beans, three different types of corn. He thought about his ninety-four-year-old grandfather back home. Grandpa Gregory would be ninety-five on Thursday. *Does a ninety-five-year-old even care about cake?*

Relly picked up the glass jar of cherries from the top shelf. He made a mental note to check them off the list as he did another fouetté. With Nita's warning still stuck in his head, Relly made sure not to stretch his leg out nearly as far. One fouetté up the aisle, then one fouetté back down. *No, let me do that again,* Relly thought. Because what harm was there in practicing another? One more fouetté down the aisle. An extra fouetté back up. By now Relly had found the pineapples.

Nita sure did keep an odd number of pineapples. Three rows packed with pineapples. Three rows stacked with pineapples. Momma wanted whole slices, big enough that when you pick up your fork, every bite of cake had a piece of fruit.

In one hand he held the jar of cherries. With the other, Relly picked up a blue-and-yellow can. Ready to turn around and meet up with his brother, his eyes shifted back to the shelf. There were the pineapples in their cans, but there was an object behind the cans that his eyes gravitated toward.

"Aye! What's up with the timber? You selling firewood now?" There was one random slim piece of wood lying on the shelf. Relly shifted the can and cherries in the palm of his hand. Then he picked up the piece of wood and held it between his thumb and pointer finger.

When he flipped it over, it warmed to his touch. Sunshining-on-your-skin type warmth. The tingling traveled up the length of his arm. From the crook of his elbow, across his shoulders, the tingling went down into his spine until it turned into a tickle that crept into his feet. Relly wiggled his toes. Relly wiggled his nose. Nita had not answered his question.

A rhythm swept into Relly's ears. It was a pulse that strummed against his eardrums until his vision began to blur. If Bobby wanted Relly to get a grip, now would have been the time.

Relly watched what looked to be the bodega tiles morphing. Underneath his sneakers, the tiles dissolved. Then they were replaced with a deep-red carpet. Above his head, the ceiling fizzled and melted into wavy lines. It turned into a solid ornate proscenium arch. The overhead lights transformed into a crystal chandelier. Aisle three was now a row of red-velvet cushiony seats. When Relly glanced behind him, each seat was occupied by folks dressed in suits and ties, fascinating tilted netted hats, and dresses etched in lace.

Relly blinked.

The shelf that used to hold pineapples vibrated so violently, Relly knew it would tumble right on top of him. It did not. Instead, the shelf slowly shifted and shrunk down into a stage. On the stage, Relly saw a man.

This man's legs moved between a walk and a dance, just as Relly had done on his way to the bodega. This man's arms swayed and swung as his legs floated into each move. He was light on his feet, agile as the smile on his face. The tapping man danced with ease, balanced and smooth. Dance converted into music through the sound from taps on his feet.

It was clear to Relly: this man on stage was breathing out a beat his ears could hear and his body could translate. Because in between the taps were slides. Slick, smooth, sleek slides. Short and sweet slides, until there was a longer slide turned glide across the entire length of the stage. If Relly didn't know any better, he would have thought there was ice underneath this man's feet.

Relly had never seen anybody on a stage do tap the way this man did tap. And the kid had seen a lot of tap. Studying the sliding, gliding, drifting man, Relly knew he could have been looking at his adult self, tapping on stage, living out his lifelong dream. Relly knew he could do those same sliding moves too.

"Relly!"

Juanita's and Bobby's voices cracked through the blur. Still, Relly's eyes only saw the same scene. The man on the stage whose name Relly had no clue of.

"Hello? Relly! Snap out of it." Bobby gripped Relly's shoulders. "First you couldn't be still. Now you're staring into space."

When Relly released the piece of wood, the images he saw were gone. Relly's eyes watered, unfocused until they landed on the can of pineapples and smashed jar of cherries on the floor.

"So much for Nita's warning." Bobby's words came out annoyed. "You know, you've got these times you don't listen. You're getting too old for that."

A wave of embarrassment swept over Relly. Bobby had

scolded him before, in their own home. Never in public. And now the store had gotten crowded since Relly went looking for pineapples and cherries. All of 132nd Street may as well have been inside Juanita's Market.

Relly bent to pick up the pineapple can. He looked at the piece of wood beside it. Bobby must not have seen what Relly saw.

"Weird," Relly said. Then he used the edge of his sweatshirt to pick up the wood. He slipped it in his pocket before Bobby could see.

"You've got a spill in the canned-food aisle!" Bobby hollered. "What's up with you today?" he asked Relly.

"Nothing is up with me. I'm good." Relly stood as Nita turned down the aisle. She tossed a roll of paper towels.

"You spill it, you clean it," Nita said as Relly caught the roll. He bent low and wiped up the mess, shooing away Harold the cat. Relly stood, balling up the wet paper towel. The two brothers headed for the front of the store.

"Good?" Bobby pointed toward the aisle. "That what you call good? I didn't think you would actually try to knock over Nita's shelf. Or her whole store. You do know you don't have to dance all the time, right? You do know there's this thing called being still?"

"I didn't actually try to knock over her shelf, Robert."

"Then what the what happened?" Bobby asked. Now

Nita was back up front. She scanned their items, minus the cherries, as Relly tossed the wet paper towel in the trash. She looked from older brother to younger brother, younger brother to older. After Bobby paid, he handed Relly the change. It never hurt to have a little extra cash before getting on the subway.

"I don't know."

"You don't know?"

"Said what I said."

"You were daydreaming."

What Relly saw felt real. Solid. Alive. Not like any daydream he ever had. But he was not about to tell that to Bobby as they walked out the bodega door. Now Relly wasn't even in the mood to dance.

"Don't tell Momma, please." Relly made his eyes wide. Bobby had never been an easy one to convince, but when his brother didn't respond, Relly knew Bobby wouldn't tell. Their momma didn't appreciate embarrassing situations. Especially if those situations involved her sons.

"I'll meet you at the Ethel after your show to take you home," Bobby said before the two brothers parted. "And try to pay attention. Get yourself together. No clumsy stuff like you did in there. What's it Grandpa's always saying?"

Relly held back rolling his eyes. *Grandpa says a lot of stuff. Grandpa's always saying too much.*

"We have to work twice as hard."

"And you know this. You're the one who made it, Relly. Don't screw it up."

The two brothers did a handshake. A closed fist. Up, then down, and a tap of their knuckles. Bobby headed back home. Relly needed to make his way to the theater for the Broadway show. But when Bobby was out of sight, Relly stopped. He dug into his pocket, closed his eyes, then pulled out the fragment of wood. It was no more than three inches thick. Smooth all around. Deep intervals of wavy brown lines dotted the piece.

"What are you?" Relly asked. He held it in his hand and squeezed tight, hoping the same scene from the bodega would pop up again. "And who was he?" Relly hoped he would see the sliding, gliding man. His legs wanted to mimic the dancing man's moves right on the street. But Relly didn't have time to spend wondering. His train would arrive in three minutes. Relly stuffed the piece of wood in his backpack, then hurtled through the crowded subway stairs.

Almost knocking over Nita's shelves was one thing. To be late to his own show and have his understudy perform, Relly would never have that.

Two

WHO'S GONNA BELIEVE ME?

Holding on to the handrail, Relly took the subway steps three at a time. Back aboveground, he squeezed in and out of the crowd, walking up Midtown's sidewalk. The aura of this part of the city hit him like a foamy ocean wave. So much to take in. Each billboard, each marquee, every flash of artificial light. Then the sounds flooded his senses too. Car honks and bikers' squeaky brakes. Shoes against pavement and a pair of headphones so loud, Relly could hear someone's calypso music.

Harlem had its noise too, but Harlem's noise came from the heart of the people. Here, in the busiest part of Manhattan, every sound, every sight seemed to have been shoved into a blender. But no amount of noise could cut out the tune that played on repeat in Relly's head.

New York, New York.

The classic Frank Sinatra song. The whole subway trip from Harlem to Midtown, Relly made up his own lyrics.

I will not be late.

Can't be late today.

I'm gonna make it on time tonight.

One time! Our Time*!*

Cutting down Forty-Fourth Street, the vibration of his phone pulsed in his pocket. Relly almost leapt across the entrance to Shubert Alley as three more vibrations came. He knew they were text messages as he reached to pull out his phone. First he peeked at the time. It was already past half hour. Past the time he was supposed to sign in. Then, unlocking his phone, he checked the messages. A slew of texts from the Squad, April, Hudson, and Monica. Relly opened Monica's first as he ran past the Broadhurst, with its wide brick columns.

M: U OK? We're worried about you. You're coming right, Relly?

R: IDK . . .

M: U don't know!??! No entiendo.

R: I mean, I am coming! I'm on my way!

M: Know u can talk to me, right? Tú estás aquí para mí, estoy aquí para ti.

Relly read Monica's text out loud. "'You're here for me. I'm here for you.'" His Spanish had gotten better over the past few months, since Monica gave Relly lessons during intermission.

M: Always.

Relly ran past the Hayes, with its dozen windows. That one always reminded Relly of a brick house squeezed between two buildings.

Always, Relly typed, until he saw the next theater up, the Ethel Merman, with its reddish-gold marquee.

R: Promise I'll tell you later, k?

There was a crowd of people who streamed their way inside. Of course there was. Relly ran around the crowd, hoping that no one would recognize him as the kid from *Our Time*. Relly usually didn't mind being recognized. But he did mind being recognized when he was late!

Call time. Relly knew at that moment the stage manager, Claudia, was checking the call-board. Checking each name of each performer, and she would not find Relly's initials. Relly could see her now, Claudia over the loudspeaker shouting, "Half hour, everyone! Relly Morton, if you are here, please let a stage manager know. And by stage manager, I mean me!"

Relly had ten minutes to be late. At 7:40, Claudia would get his understudy, Jacob, ready. A notice would be put in the program that Relly would not perform as Pax tonight. Then they would replace his headshot in the front lobby with Jacob's, and if fans had come to see Relly and only Relly, hello, hello, surprise, surprise!

"I will not be late today," Relly said as he slid around the side of the building, dodging a dog walker with four Boston terriers on a leash. "Cute dogs!" He nodded to the walker, easing his way closer to the stage-door entrance.

"I will not be late."

The train hadn't come on time. Not the A train. Not the 2. Not the C or the D. Not even the 3. Each one was late, which meant Relly was late. Which meant when Relly ran into Jimmy Onions, the Ethel's stage-door doorman, his words finally caught up with him.

"Hate to break it to ya, kid. You're late," Jimmy said as he held the stage door open. After forty-four years of service at the now-infamous theater, Jimmy still had the perfect sense of timing. Sure, his security camera helped. Knowing the job helped too.

"I know!" The click of the door behind Relly made his lateness finite. He hoped for some type of relief. Relief for how out of breath he now felt, having run across half of Times Square. Relief to take away the guilt hovering above his shoulders. He could not let the Squad down. Relly scribbled his initials on the call-board against the wall.

When he quickly checked the time again, it was now seven forty-five.

"Maybe she won't notice." Relly nodded to the board. "Right?" He put the dry-erase marker on the table. "It's only fifteen minutes."

Jimmy took a bite of a green apple, sat himself in the seat next to the door, and said through a full mouth, "Fifteen minutes before showtime." Jimmy swallowed. "Oh, she'll notice, Relly Morton. Long as you've been here, don't you know Claudia never fails to notice?" Claudia Middleton, stage manager, noticed *everything*.

The Ethel Merman Theater, named after the famed Ethel Merman, was small but peculiar, tiny yet robust. The ornate building on the rim of Broadway gave off the feeling of *Anything Goes*. Ethel sang it in the 1934 Broadway hit by the same name.

Times have changed,
and we've often rewound the clock!

Inside, the theater showed no sign of last year's curse. The curse that stunk up the Ethel Merman worse than a Florida swamp. The curse that caused its walls to peel and sets to break. But the people, that curse got to them, too, stealing away their talents. Their joy.

It finally ceased when Monica Garcia, who played Tony in *Our Time*, unlocked a plan to get rid of the abomination placed upon the Ethel. Of course, the Squad, the name given to the four cast members by their director, Artie Hoffman, helped along the way.

Relly ran past Jimmy and his apple, up a flight of stairs, down an almost-empty hallway to the wood-paneled dressing room he shared with Hudson. Hudson played Crash in *Our Time*. Normally, the two got ready together, but Hudson was nowhere in sight as Relly pulled his costume off the hanger and jumped inside the clothes. Then, Relly left the dressing room and ran down the hall again, this time around the corner to the wig room. In the room with the long mirrors and longer tables, Chris stood with a comb between his teeth, styling a short-haired wig. He didn't even look up when Relly entered.

"You've been waiting for me?"

"Not like you to be late." Chris grabbed the brown-haired wig with the sharp part from the table. He quickly fit the wig to Relly's head. "Good thing I always have a backup. You think your understudy is going to be happy about this? Jacob was more excited than my three-year-old granddaughter at the M&M's store when he found out he would be performing tonight."

"I know! I know!" When Relly squeezed and tugged the wig onto his head, he caught a glimpse of himself in the mirror. "I mean, no, he won't be happy. He's going to fume!" Yup, his understudy would be furious. Jacob never took kindly to getting his Broadway dreams dashed. Relly doubled-checked his look in the mirror. Costume, check. Shoes, check. Hair, check. Not a peek of Relly's purple-and-pink-dyed hair showed underneath.

"I'll say a little prayer for you."

"Forever?" Relly asked, thinking of the song Momma liked to sing.

"And ever," Chris said as Relly left the dressing room and found himself running down the hall again. Only this time he was headed backstage.

"Five!" Claudia called through the speaker. "Five!"

"Thank you, five!" echoed throughout the Ethel Merman. Up ahead, Relly could see April, Monica, and Hudson in a wing of the stage behind the curtain. April and Monica were both stretching with foam rollers on the floor. Hudson quit his vocal warm-up the moment he saw Relly.

"Finally!" he said, nodding to a lingering actor a few feet away. Jacob. Hudson lifted his thumb in a backward motion. At that moment, Jacob removed his headphones. The understudy tapped his phone, cutting his music. Jacob huffed. Jacob scuffed. Relly swore he saw his understudy stomp his left foot against the hardwood.

"Uhn! I was getting in the correct headspace." His shoes squeaked against the backstage floor. "I can't believe

Claudia is still letting you go on this close to showtime, Relly." Jacob side-eyed Relly as he removed himself from backstage. "Thanks. A. Lot!"

Hudson looked physically relieved. "Jacob is cool and all, but he never has the timing right. He's always off by half a second, and half a second may as well be half a minute. That's a big deal."

"Dude, what happened to you? We literally thought you weren't coming. Hudson even texted you. Did you get Hudson's text? Did you get my text? Did you get Monica's text?" April didn't look up from her foam roller on the floor.

"Yes, I got your texts," Relly said as he watched April hold out her phone, filming a quick story for Insta. Relly saw her type #backstagelife.

"Places!" Claudia called over the speaker. "Places, everyone! Relly Morton, good grief, finally. You're here."

Who's gonna believe me? Relly thought as he watched Monica stand and stretch her arms above her head. She held the stretch several seconds before turning her head left to right. Monica caught Relly's eye and stopped. The two friends often shared glances. They could know what each other was thinking without saying a word.

"Want to talk about it?" Monica whispered. "After the show? Te sentirás mejor pronto!"

Relly nodded. It would make him feel better to tell his

friends what had happened at the bodega, but now was not the time. Not right before their performance. Not when they all needed to get in the right headspace. The info Relly had to unveil needed time to be digested. He would tell Monica and the rest of the Squad later.

Places.

Relly inhaled, letting adrenaline move through his body. From each hair on his head to the tips of his toes. Adrenaline settled in his veins. It moved through his muscles. Relly's senses kicked in. The audience that was chatty five seconds ago quieted. The lights lowered. Over a speaker came a voice: "Ladies and gentlemen, welcome to the Ethel Merman Theater. Quiet your cell phones and sit back for a ride. Enjoy *Our Time*."

It was time. Their time to perform. This was the moment Relly worked half his twelve-year-old life for. *Our Time*.

The Squad started with the opening song. The musical played tribute to 1980s movies. A time when adventure flashed on movie screens. Relly, April, Monica, and Hudson brought that same adventure to the stage. Soon came the jumps and chases. A tomato fight between pirouettes and relevés, backflips and a leap from an artificial fifteen-foot waterfall onstage.

When it came to the scene Relly and Hudson shared, Relly always felt it was truly his time. A series of moves escaped from the half-moon-shaped taps on their shoes. Relly could feel the audience's captivation as he and Hudson showed off. Triple-time steps, ball change, shuffle off to Buffalo against the orchestra music. Beneath their taps came the sounds.

Te. Te. Te. Ta.

Tee, tee. Tee, tee, ta.

Tee. Tee. Tee. Ta.

Beneath his feet, then

Silence.

But when he was supposed to ease from the double Cincinnati, a tap move that called for Relly to lift his heels and shuffle his feet in double the time, Relly found himself sliding, gliding from left wing to right. All the way across the stage, Relly eased on the edges of his taps. He hadn't planned to do the move, and it was not a move in the show. But Relly felt he had no control over his body. And once he finished the first slide, Relly knew he had to do another, and another, and one more. Across the stage, back and forth. Sliding, gliding, backward, forward. Exactly like the man he saw at the bodega.

April and Monica stood in the wings, wide-eyed, open-mouthed. Hudson, still onstage, stood frozen in a panicked shock.

"What are you doing, Relly? That is not part of the

show!" Hudson whispered through clenched teeth. He smacked his forehead with his palm before showing the same tight, toothy smile to the audience. Hudson kept up with his own moves, tapping in twice the time to make up for Relly's mishap.

And when the moment wore off, Relly came back to his regular position as if nothing had happened. Just in time for the barrel roll. An intense silence filled the theater. From the balcony to the orchestra seats to the front lobby. Relly knew even Jimmy sat in silence at the stage door, watching on his tiny TV. Then the audience's quiet merged into a gush of praise. Applause and whoops. Hoots, hollers, and feet stomps. A child in the front row screamed, "Do that again! Do that again!" Clearly, the audience loved it.

Back in the dressing room, Relly hung up his costume and took off his wig. Chris would be in to get it later. That thrill still coursed through him, as the closing number was still stuck in Relly's head. Relly turned around and did a simple kick ball change. It was a kick of his right foot, then a step out, and a step back with his left. The move was the perfect way to end the night. The perfect step to get out the rest of his adrenaline and guilt for being late.

"You could have warned me, ya know. Seriously. I don't mind surprises, but I do mind surprises onstage in front of hundreds of people with all eyes on us. Give me a heads-up next time you decide to do a new move, Relly," Hudson said, holding a green-and-white glass tray. Hudson baked treats for every show. Inside were only crumbs left over from his cookies.

"Sorry," Relly said. "You remember how your pants split on opening night? Remember how you didn't know that would happen? It was kind of like that."

Hudson shrugged. "If you say so. It's over. Hey, I would have saved you some cookies earlier, but the longer I waited, the more you didn't show. Then tech came in and asked if they could have a cookie, and before I knew it, poof! They were gone! My mom brought this tray all the way from Goa. It was my grandma's. Think it'll look nice on FoodTube?"

Hudson's *Broadway Sizzlers* video series had been a hit. Since *Our Time* turned into the megashow of the season, Hudson had octuple the views since his first episode. He even started to get special requests from Broadway stars to make guest appearances.

"Leslie Odom Jr.!" Hudson screamed to Relly over the phone two months ago. "Can you believe *the* Leslie Odom Jr. wants to be on *my* cooking show? I'm gonna faint!" Yes, Relly could believe it. Hudson's food was that good.

Relly peeked into the empty glass container. Out of the

corner of his eye, he spotted April and Monica standing at the dressing-room door.

April played Froggie in *Our Time*. She still talked as if her mind would run out of things to say. April held up her phone, once again on Insta. Relly stood and grabbed his coat as April turned ever so slightly, taking a panoramic photo of the room.

"Mind if I show my fans your digs?" April said, already typing another hashtag into the caption box. *#dressingroomdigs #dotheyevenknowhowtocleanup?* *#ourdressingroomisbetter* "There's a million people out there. Dare I say two million?"

April was talking about the people outside the stage door. The crowd that patiently, or impatiently, waited for autographs. Relly could guarantee half that crowd would be for April. One of her goals at the start of *Our Time* was to get more followers. She had no problem doing that. It ballooned from ten thousand in November to twenty thousand by December to thirty thousand, where it's been holding steady.

"I'm not trying to be an influencer. I'm really not. But if people want to see how Broadway is done, what better way than to see it through me?" April told them over pizza in Brooklyn one day a month ago when they wanted to get away. "You know who started following me yesterday? Michelle Obama!"

It was true; Relly checked.

Hudson got up to join April and Monica. Relly grabbed his backpack, taking a quick peek inside. He looked up to make sure his friends weren't watching. They weren't. Hudson was too busy trying to get April to take the crumbs from the Tupperware tray.

The sliver of wood, his newest possession, was still tucked inside. Safe.

"You coming, Relly?" Monica asked.

"On my way!"

Relly lifted his backpack, hearing the taps April made on her phone. It chimed each time she accepted a new follower. As Relly reached the door, Monica gave Relly a smile. The understudy turned Broadway star had almost gotten out of the habit of twisting the brown curls on top of her head. It was a nervous habit, and Relly hadn't seen her do it for at least three months. But today the habit was back.

Monica from California came to *Our Time* through a video audition. She originally came as an understudy to the understudy, until the curse called her to the leading role as Tony. Now she and her abuelita lived in Brooklyn, in a rented blue-and-white row house with curved windows. When her family came to visit from Cali, the Squad always met up for pizza.

The person Relly hadn't noticed behind April and Monica was Claudia Middleton.

"You three head out. I need a word with Mr. Morton." The Ethel stage manager stepped forward. Her thick shoes sounded off against the hallway tile. April, Monica, and Hudson stared in a bewildered silence as Claudia nodded to the room Relly was on the verge of leaving.

"Now?"

"Now, Mr. Morton." When the stage manager walked inside, Monica mouthed, *You need help? I got your back. Siempre.*

Relly shook his head. He could handle this on his own.

"Did Hudson forget to save you a cookie?" Relly asked as he sat at the vanity. He turned the small seat around to face the stage manager.

"No. He. Did. Not. Matter of fact." Claudia shook her shoulders, smoothing out her black blouse. "I don't understand why I'm always the last person to get any of his treats." Claudia shook her head as if to shake off the thought. "But that's not why I'm here. I'm here, Relly Morton, because twice today you did not bring your personal best."

There was the distinct sound of shuffling in the hallway. Squeaky shoes against the tile. Quiet whispers from the Squad. His friends were eavesdropping.

"Those puppy eyes might work on your brother; they

will not work on me." Claudia pulled a notebook from her pocket. She flipped through several pages before stopping at one page scribbled with line after line of notes.

"Let's see here. Instance one occurred at seven forty-five and seven seconds this evening. You were distractingly late. So late, we had to get your understudy ready." Claudia continued before Relly could respond. "Instance two occurred onstage at approximately nine thirty-eight. You performed a series of slides. Which were good. Matter of fact, they were incredible." Claudia paused. "But they, as in those slides, were not supposed to be in the show. Relly, what is wrong? And tell me how I can help you today."

"Nothing's wrong."

"You sure? You seem distracted, yes? You are rattled today, yes? Off your game, correct?"

"No. I am not rattled."

"My first question."

"I'm not distracted, either."

"My last question?"

"No! I'm not off my game."

Claudia sighed.

"It was a semi-accident."

"A semi-what, now?"

"I didn't mean to be late. You know the trains in this city. And the move just came to me."

"It just came to you?"

"Yes."

Claudia stood and pocketed her notebook. Again, she smoothed out her blouse as she stepped to the door. "Semi-accident or not. You have three chances, Relly. You've already used two today."

"Two? What do you mean I've used two?" Relly asked. He took in a deep inhale as he stood, trying to catch his breath. "When I use up the last one, then what happens?"

Sure, he had been a few minutes late before, but never enough for his understudy to get ready. Sure, he had almost forgotten moves onstage, but never actually performed the wrong ones. Until today. Relly followed Claudia into the hallway. April, Monica, and Hudson scrambled down the hall.

"I call in your understudy. Permanently."

At the entrance of his dressing room, a sinking feeling settled in the back of his throat. It tingled from Relly's fingertips. It went to his veins, then up his arm, then down his spine, until the feeling reached his feet. That feeling consumed him. At twelve, Relly didn't have to wait until he was an adult to reach his dreams. Each day his feet slipped on tap shoes, each time they tapped off, then back onto the floor again, Relly was living his dream.

Could all that be taken away? All because he was a little distracted?

The Squad felt the cool New York wind sneak its way through the crack under the stage door. They could hear the cheers and chants outside. Excitement coursed through the air into the Ethel Merman as Relly zipped up his coat. Jimmy smiled, giving Relly a fist bump.

"Thought I'd have to come and find you."

April, Monica, and Hudson had waited for Relly to return from his talk with Claudia. Now they stood inside the stage door. All four waited for Jimmy to give a rundown on what to expect before they stepped out to sign autographs.

"Here's the scoop: We've got twenty-two families requesting autographs. The entire sixth, seventh, and eighth grades from Harlem School of the Arts. There's a five-year-old who will not stop asking if I got my name from the vegetable, and ten groups of teens dressed up as Pax, Crash, Froggie, and Tony. Think you can handle that?"

"Not a problem for me," Relly said. He always looked for the fans dressed up in costume as his character, Pax.

"Harlem School of the Arts!" Monica bounced up and down on her tiptoes. She did a little clap, reminiscent of her abuelita's reaction when she heard something she liked. "Jimmy, we've handled more people than this on our slowest days."

"We want the Squad! Give us the Squad!" their fans shouted outside. "Where is the Squad? Come out Squad!"

"Sounds like mutiny out there," said Hudson.

"Sounds like I'm about to gain some followers," added April as Monica stretched each finger before grabbing a Sharpie off the table. Then Jimmy opened the door. A gust of wind stomped inside the Ethel as April, Monica, and Hudson exited. Relly attempted to follow his friends, but before he could step foot over the threshold, the same one that still held the penny above the doorframe, Jimmy stepped in front of him.

"Got you rattled, huh?" Jimmy asked. His two thick eyebrows gave him a concerned, contemplative look.

"Huh? You talking about me being late?" Relly tried to peek around the doorman. "Are you talking about Claudia?" He could see the Squad steadily make their way down the line of people holding out *Playbill*s and posing for photographs. At that moment, Relly heard a fan shout, "Hey! You're missing someone. Where's Pax?"

"Not in the slightest." Jimmy shook his head. "Claudia will be fine, Relly. I've seen thousands of people come in and out this stage door. I know the look of an actor startled. When you popped up earlier, you had a look worse than somebody who's seen a real live ghost. You've seen some-thin', kid. If you want to talk, you know where to find me."

Jimmy stepped aside, out of Relly's way. Relly took a step outside too, away from the door. "Jimmy!" Relly yelled as his voice was overpowered by the crowd and their shouts.

"Pax! Pax!" Their yells erupted against Relly's ears.

"Jimmy!"

"Pax! Pax! Pax!"

Jimmy stood outside the stage door. It was his job to make sure the Squad stayed safe. But now Jimmy was in a deep conversation, giving a fan directions. No mat-ter how many times Relly tried to get Jimmy's attention, Relly's words were overpowered and submerged under-neath the voice of the crowd. Relly stood there, watching Jimmy, contemplating if he should tell Jimmy what he saw before he told Monica and the rest of the Squad. Finally, Hudson dragged Relly up the line. Relly would have to talk to Jimmy another time.

Three

GRANDPA GREGORY

The crowd leaned against the barricades as the Squad walked their red carpet. Fans held out *Playbill*s, jumping up and down. Every few people, Relly saw fans with headshots for April, Hudson, himself, and Monica to sign. Even though all four were wiped out, exhausted after the two-hour show, the Squad signed each item. April even signed a fan's arm. She did not miss a single photo flash as she shook hands and waved to fans on Insta Live. The barricades may have separated the Squad from their fans, but it was clear if a fan could get any closer, they would.

"Hashtag 'photo-op.' Hashtag 'call me Froggie.' Hashtag 'best part of Broadway is the fans.'"

"Hashtag 'will we ever run out of hashtags?'" Hudson walked past April to catch up with Relly. Relly handed a signed *Playbill* back to the five-year-old Jimmy had mentioned.

"Hashtag 'cute kid,'" Relly replied, taking a poster from a fan. He scribbled his signature, thinking about what Jimmy had said at the stage door. Relly did need to talk. He needed to know what he had found in the bodega and why it had been waiting for him. Relly needed to know the name of the man he had seen sliding on a stage. But how could Jimmy or the Squad possibly know an answer to that?

"Thirty minutes and done!" Relly signed his last autograph. "That didn't take me near as long as Saturday night. Remember when we were out here past midnight? Bobby was mad. I mean, swear I saw steam come out his ears. Older brothers. Geesh. They are so moody." Relly looked up to see if his brother was at the end of the line. He wasn't, yet.

"As an older brother, younger brothers can be . . . what's the word?" Hudson paused to think. "Agaçant."

"Did you just call me annoying in French?"

"N-no," stammered Hudson. "I meant the collective younger brother. Very bothersome. Do not recommend."

As Relly and Hudson made it to the end of the line, April and Monica stood waiting. Relly contemplated what it would take for April and Monica to spill their *Playbill*-signing secrets. A lifetime supply of Hudson's treats? Relly's prized poster signed by Savion Glover? Hudson's treats and the poster signed by Savion Glover? To be a fast signer was a mystery Relly always wanted to figure out.

As the crowd dispersed, Hudson gathered closer to April and Monica. Relly saw Hudson take a large inhale of air. Then Hudson looked from April to Monica and back to Relly as he let that air out.

"We need to talk to you." Hudson inhaled again. It sounded as if he sucked up all the air in all New York State.

"Is this about your cookies?"

"This is not about my cookies!"

"'Cause I'm not mad you didn't have any left."

Hudson looked back to Monica, who looked to April, who nodded for Hudson to continue. When Hudson shook his head, he inhaled one last time. Then Monica spoke up instead.

"Everybody including Jacob was waiting to see if you would be a no-show. What's going on? Qué pasó? Is everything all right with you today?"

"Yeah!" Relly said with a cough.

"You seem a little off tonight," said Monica.

"A little?" Hudson rolled his eyes.

"Me. Off? No way!" Relly laughed, but the Squad did not laugh back.

"Here's the deal: You're normally on, Relly. Out of all of us, you pull us together. You help us get our act right. But, Relly, tonight that was not the case."

"April's right. I don't think I've ever seen you so absent-minded," said Monica.

"You tried out a new move!" Hudson shouted. He lowered his voice before a lingering fan could hear. "What was I supposed to do except stand there in the middle of the show looking ridiculous? That's almost as bad as me splitting my pants opening night. Which I never want to be reminded of, by the way."

"You can talk to us anytime," Monica added. "You can talk to me anytime," she said a little lower. "Remember our text?"

"I'm not off." Relly gripped the straps of his backpack. He tugged twice.

Am I? Relly thought. How could he explain what he had done onstage? Tap moves that came to him out the blue. Moves that didn't belong in the show. Moves not even his own, but they somehow found their way to his legs. How could he explain to his friends he had seen a man tapping and sliding on an imaginary stage at a bodega in the middle of Harlem?

"Is this some type of intervention?" Relly asked.

"No way!" Hudson shouted.

April nodded. "We're making sure you're all good."

"What April said. We want to make sure it won't happen again," Monica added.

"Ever," Hudson emphasized. "How much trouble did you get into?"

"Third strike and Claudia's calling in my understudy. Permanently."

Monica gasped. April and Hudson stared in surprise as Relly studied the sidewalk. Relly was glad that when he looked up, Bobby stood on the opposite side of the barricade.

"All done?"

Relly nodded as his brother gave a hurried wave. "Big bro's here," Relly said. He really didn't want to see the look of disappointment on the Squad's faces. "See you next show. I'll be on time, promise!" Relly sped past his friends, hopping over the barricade. He didn't look back. That promise was one promise Relly did not know if he could keep.

The Morton apartment sat in the basement of Vanderzee Heights. It was a twenty-seven-story apartment building in the middle of 119th Street. At the front entrance, each brown brick towered above him. Relly remembered when he used to attempt cartwheels up and down the stairs. Behind him was the park, where he remembered dance battles with the kids from his building.

But it was the Morton apartment that held the most memories. Relly's and Bobby's shoes echoed between the walls as they stepped inside. The steel door slammed shut behind them. The sound echoed as Relly inhaled the smell of Pine-Sol and lemon. Mrs. Lewis up on floor four loathed a dusty entryway. As they walked forward and rounded the corner for the stairs, Relly was reminded of their dad.

Daddy used to scoop Relly up and carry Relly on his shoulders when they came home. As Relly and Bobby walked down one flight of stairs, Relly remembered his dad planting kisses on the top his head. Daddy used to whisper in Relly's ear.

Little man! Little man!

Relly wasn't so little anymore. Still, some days Daddy's voice reverberated in Relly's mind so loud, Relly could have sworn he was right beside him.

You're on your way to the stars, Rel! Daddy used to say. *Don't let a thing stop you.*

As Relly and Bobby walked through the front door of apartment 3, the smell of barbeque chicken and baked potatoes greeted their nostrils. An icy pitcher of peppermint water stood on the kitchen countertop. The murmur of Momma's television reached through to the living room as "Lovely Day" by Bill Withers played on the radio. Radio or no radio, Relly missed his dad's voice.

"Momma, play it from your cell phone," Relly suggested, closing the apartment door. Relly's momma eased from the hallway to the living room. She wore a black-and-gold scarf tied across her head. The knot at the top always looked like a flower about to bud. The way Momma tied the scarf was magic. Fingers lacing, twisting, pulling to create the knot.

"Listen, baby, you like music from that phone, I like music from my radio," Momma said as she turned the dial. Each turn made a distinctive click, tick, click.

"Don't you hear that?"

"Hear what?" both sons asked.

"Music that's got heart. That's how it's supposed to sound. Music was meant to be played from radios; that's why they were invented."

Now Momma moved her arms to snuggle both sons. In that tight hug, she looked them in their eyes as if tonight were the first time she'd seen them in months. Relly didn't mind the snuggles, but he didn't show he didn't mind. Instead, he put on a front, exactly like his brother. The two tried to escape Momma's tight squeeze.

"Barbecue's in the oven. Mac and cheese's on the stove. Don't either one of you stay up past one. You're cranky when you get no sleep, and you know this."

"Momma." Relly pouted. It was a pout that said he would rather have her own cooking. Even though Momma always brought food home from the diner as a treat, Relly thought Momma's cooking tasted better. Fresher. The best.

Momma did a shimmy, clapping her hands and snapping her fingers to the beat. When she sang, it was her version of "Lovely Day" that escaped her mouth. All the lovely days combined to meet and join on this Tuesday, almost Wednesday, night, almost morning. Relly moonwalked from the front door, across the living room to the dining room, which combined into one big room. He lifted his heels off the floor and did a spin next to the dining room table.

"Show-off." Bobby watched as Relly dropped his heels.

"Not my fault you have two left feet." Relly tapped his toes. "Not my fault you don't have my dancing gene." Relly moved his legs so they were hopscotching, double-Dutching without any rope. It was a move made famous by John Bubbles, the Black tap dancer known for rhythm, heel, and toe tap. Relly's arms moved along with his feet because they were part of the dance too. Bobby tried to match Relly's steps, but Bobby looked more like a robot on ice than any Broadway performer.

"I'll stick with engineering school," Bobby said with a mouthful of potatoes. All month he had been working on his college applications.

"Bet." Relly held out his hand and made a fist. Bobby

tapped his fist to Relly's. "And I'll stick with dancing, 'cause we all know that's something you can't do." True. Bobby's moves were worse than any robot's.

Relly wondered how much Bobby knew about the bodega incident. He had been there, yes. He had seen Relly stand frozen in the middle of the aisle. He had seen the crushed jar of cherries on the floor tile. But Relly was not sure Bobby had seen the store morph. Bobby hadn't remotely mentioned a stage, or seats and people dressed to the nines. There had been no mention of the man who tapped and slid and slid and tapped, owning that stage.

Momma kissed Relly's forehead before she went down the hall. She rubbed the top of Relly's head in a series of forward motions. Momma smoothed his hair that had gotten frizzy from the wig into flat, delicate waves.

"Don't stay up too late." Momma yawned as she walked into her bedroom; at that same moment, Bobby went to his. "That's the last time I'm going to tell the both of you." When neither brother said a word, Momma hollered, "I know I'm not talking to myself."

"I won't!" Relly hollered back.

"Won't what?" Momma asked.

"Stay up late," the brothers replied.

"Good. Love you both," Momma told them.

Now, with Bobby and Momma gone, Relly sat at the

kitchen table with the plate of food from Nora's Diner. The sliver of wood was still in his backpack hanging from the kitchen chair. He envisioned the piece of wood right next to his tap shoes. The longer it sat at the bottom of his bag, the more Relly had the urge to take it out and have one more look. Relly resisted as he bit into his food and stared at the coffeepot on the table.

It broke over a month ago. Momma hadn't been able to fix her morning coffee when it steamed and sputtered. Relly hadn't hesitated to say he would fix it. Between the leaky faucet and the microwave that cut off in the middle of cooking, Relly wanted to fix everything. When he tried to treat for dinner, or pay a bill, or fix broken appliances around the house, Momma refused. She told Relly it wouldn't be right for a mother to take money from her own son. Relly's money was Relly's money for him to save, not to use up.

"You reckoning with that contraption again?" said a voice from the living room. Relly jumped in his seat, almost knocking over the empty coffeepot and his food. He thought he was in this part of the apartment alone. Guess everyone hadn't gone to bed.

"Grandpa!" Relly got up from his seat and rushed over to give his grandfather a hug. Usually, each night when Relly came home, Grandpa Gregory was sound asleep. Not tonight. Grandpa Gregory's eyes were wide as Relly sat back at the table to finish his plate.

"Could've sworn I saw you working on that thing last week round this time."

"I was, Grandpa," Relly said as he dropped back into his seat. "Wanna help me fix it?"

Grandpa Gregory shifted from his spot on the couch. Relly couldn't tell if he was moving because he wanted to get up, or if he was moving because his body ached. Grandpa Gregory's body always ached.

"What you need to do is go out and buy a new one. You can buy better than what you can fix, Relly." Of course, they could go out and buy a new coffeepot if Momma didn't have her pride. Plus, wasn't there a little bit of fun in trying to fix an old one? Relly looked at Grandpa on the couch.

Grandpa Gregory was tall. Much taller than Relly. One inch taller than Bobby. The way Gregory's body leaned off the couch made the piece of furniture look like it didn't belong. Plus, Gregory was slim. But he hadn't always been that way. Grandpa Gregory used to move. His legs and arms used to hold muscle. Today, Grandpa Gregory Morton couldn't move like he used to. Not with the way arthritis attacked his body, climbed through each joint, freezing the bones in place.

"Y'all get a crowd tonight?"

"Sold out! You should have seen the line for autographs. Thought we'd be all night signing. Lost count how many kids I saw dressed up as Pax."

"That your character?"

"Uh-huh." Relly took a bite of his potato.

"What's that number your momma likes? The one she talks about all the time." Grandpa Gregory snapped his fingers, trying to recall the beat. "Sing a bit for me." Grandpa closed his eyes, waiting for Relly to answer.

"'Growin' Up in the 'Burbs'?"

"That one sounds right."

Relly inhaled, and quickly let the air out. He tried to gather up any energy he could find to do a mini performance at one in the morning.

"Growin' up in the 'burbs, they all think we're disturbed, we're never quiet and neat . . ."

It wasn't as it would have been onstage. Not this late as Relly stood next to the kitchen table and danced out the routine. Grandpa Gregory had never seen *Our Time*.

"Would you look at that?" Grandpa did a jump-clap on the couch. He winced even as he did that small move. Then he hummed along with Relly's melody. "Your momma tell you I'm looking forward to seeing your show Thursday night? My Relly up on a Broadway stage! Boy oh boy." Grandpa clapped his hands as he sat up straight. He looked his grandson in the eyes.

"If your father could see you perform, I declare he would be bursting proud."

"Yeah, Momma said the same thing when I got cast," Relly said, trying to keep the conversation off his father as he sat at the table. His dad had never gotten the chance to see him perform.

"Good." Grandpa adjusted another pillow. He held it in his hand before tossing it to the end of the couch. "Listen, you been thinking about what I asked you the other night? Finding a backup plan. An alternative, son."

"An alternative to what? I already have an understudy." Relly thought back to Claudia and her warning. It gave him a chill almost as bad as thinking about the Harlem bodega shifting into a theater.

"Alternative to Broadway. All that dancing and singing, jazz and whatnot. You expect to make it a career that lasts?" Grandpa humphed, closing his eyes as he recalled, "I'll be ninety-five this Thursday. The years go by fast, Relly. Before you know it, wham-bam, your whole life has flashed by."

Grandpa's words made Relly's heart pulse in sync with the soukous African beat three floors up. Those same words made Relly's underarms sweat worse than the leaky faucet on the bathroom tub. Even his feet got itchy. Happened when he got nervous or upset. Getting nervous rarely happened for Relly.

"A backup plan never hurt nobody, especially when the fans start to fade. Those fans will start to fade."

"I don't think my fans are going anywhere."

"Humph," Grandpa let out again. "You could follow your brother when he gets into tech school. Now that's the ticket: follow Robert Morton's lead. Engineering, Relly. Ever thought 'bout that?"

No.

The thought of doing anything other than dance filled Relly's body with an intense sadness. The same sadness he had when he found out his father had passed. To not dance would be to lose a piece of himself forever.

"When I dance, I fly, Grandpa. When I fly, nothing can knock me down. If I didn't dance, I think I would sink."

"Say what, now?"

Relly got up from the table. He scraped the remnants of his food into the trash and opened the dishwasher. Relly put the plate inside. He closed the dishwasher and pushed the rinse button.

"No, Grandpa, I haven't thought about being an engineer." He mumbled under this breath, "Until right this second."

"There's all types of camps and programs and workshops and whatnot for kids your age. Tech workshops, Rel. Now, with your brother and his brain, that's double the chance for you try something new. Something solid."

Grandpa's words got caught in Relly's head. Because, what if Grandpa was right? Weren't grandparents always right? Relly had been late, which had never happened before. He had done a new move onstage, something he had never done before. Claudia could be right, too. *Am I off? I was seeing things earlier! Do I need a backup plan? What is happening to me?*

"I hear you, Grandpa." Relly turned out the kitchen light.

"Do you, now? Or you just saying that to get me to hush my mouth? Listen, I'm only trying to protect my grandson." Grandpa leaned back and closed his eyes. "'Cause I know."

Relly felt his grandfather's protection, but he didn't understand the reason behind Grandpa Gregory's words.

"This industry isn't kind to everyone, son. Hear me out, will you?"

"I'll look into it," Relly said. By the time he got to his bedroom, Relly could hear Grandpa Gregory snoring.

Six o'clock in the morning, Relly exited the rooftop door and walked to his favorite spot, the wooden bench. It sat between two knee-length terra-cotta pots. At one point they both had held light orange snapdragons and purple cosmos with yellow centers. Early Wednesday morning, those pots didn't even hold dirt. The rooftop garden had been cleared out ages ago. Relly sat on the wooden bench and let his fingers hover over five carved letters.

Daddy.

Relly had carved the name in the bench four years after his father passed. Four years after the last time his dad had taken him up on the rooftop to water plants. Back then it had been a lush oasis, a botanical garden above Harlem's own skyscraper of homes. Relly tried to remember, were his dad's eyes light brown, or dark? Were his palms rough when they used to hold hands? Or smooth? Did his dad's voice come out soft as the black-and-gold silk scarf Momma wore? The building front door shut twenty-seven floors down.

Or rough as the door slam?

Relly pulled his phone from his back pocket. After his conversation with Grandpa and before crawling into bed, he had sent Monica, April, and Hudson a text. **Can we talk?** But none of them had responded to the late-night text. As a last resort, Relly had even sent a text to his brother.

Relly: Meet me @ the rooftop. 6AM!

His older brother hadn't responded to the text Relly sent

either. Typical Bobby. Relly clicked on his playlist named "Syncopation." One word that meant a slew of rhythms combined to make one new sound. The pianist, Jelly Roll, erupted from his phone. Notes of piano jazz spread across the rooftop. Relly usually came up on the roof to think or gain a moment of peace from Bobby. Some days, he came up there to feel twenty-seven stories closer to his dad.

Relly got up and let the balls of his feet lift and rise. Front to back, back to front. His shoes slid against the rooftop concrete, as if they were sliding on ice or slipping on water. He mimicked the moves of the dancing man. Whoever the man he had seen at the bodega was, to Relly it had looked like there had been an invisible magic carpet placed underneath his feet.

The rooftop door opened, then slammed shut. Relly didn't bother to look behind him. He kept dancing, kept leaning into his moves, stolen from the dancing man. From the base of his neck, Relly knew he was being watched. *Let him watch,* Relly thought.

"Six on a Wednesday morning? Really, Relly?" Bobby asked, placing his hands together in three slow claps. Relly turned to see his brother step over to the bench and take a seat. Bobby hadn't even brushed his hair yet.

"I don't remember the last time I was up at six in the morning. Or seven. Or eight."

"Or nine," Relly added. "How do you expect to go to college?"

"I'll be all good by then, Rel. Don't you worry." Bobby rubbed sleep from his eyes. "I'll be an expert early-morning waker-upper."

"Welp, there's a first time for everything." Relly sat beside his brother on the bench. Once again, his fingers hovered over those five carved letters.

"Whatever you want better be good." Bobby let out a deep yawn. Relly stared off across the rooftop to the rest of Harlem. Rooftop after rooftop after rooftop and brick buildings. The sun started to rise across New York City.

"What's up? 'Cause I've got a bed that's warm and a pillow calling my first, middle, and last names."

Relly took in a deep breath. Just as he had let his dance flow minutes before Bobby arrived, Relly let his words loose.

"What if I'm doing the wrong thing? What if I'm not supposed to dance? What if I mess up again and Claudia kicks me out of the show and I let the Squad down, and I let Momma down and Daddy, too? 'Cause Daddy's always watching, right? And Grandpa's been saying I should find something else to do. Some type of backup plan. Like I'm a flash drive for a computer, but I'm not a flash drive, Bobby. Am I a flash drive? No! I'm me! But what if Grandpa is right and I'm the one who's wrong?"

Bobby let out a laugh that echoed across the rooftop. A pigeon jolted and flew off the ledge. When he saw that Relly was serious, Bobby closed his mouth and cut his laugh short.

"You for real? You being serious right now?"

Relly tilted his head to the right. He raised both eyebrows and nodded.

"Look, you're the best dancer in Harlem. You've got skill, Relly. None of that is going to go away, no matter if you're in a show or not. In *Our Time* or not. Or a stage or dancing in Juanita's bodega. It's in you, Relly, no matter what. That's on that."

Is it, though? Still, Relly nodded at his brother's words, taking in another deep breath. He ran his fingers along the carved name.

"Noted."

"I hope so. You having some type of twelve-year-old crisis?"

"No," Relly said. "I mean yes." He shook his head. "I mean no. No. Yes!" Relly stood again. "I hear you. But you're the one going to tech school."

"It's called MIT. Massachusetts Institute of Technology."

"Right." Relly nodded. "You're the one who doesn't need an al-ter-na-tive." Relly tapped out each syllable with his feet. "You're the one who doesn't need a back-up-plan." Relly tapped those three syllables, too.

"Grandpa is getting in your head. Rule number one about Grandpa Gregory: Do not let him get in your head." Bobby put an arm around Relly's shoulders. Finally, Relly was still. "But look. You want to be in crisis mode and figure out a backup plan, which you do not need, I got you. You're my little brother. I always got you. Want me to see what I can do about finding tech workshops for kids your age round here?"

Relly nodded as Bobby stood. His older brother headed for the rooftop door, leaving Relly on the bench. Relly rubbed his fingers against the five carved letters one more time.

"You need any more answers, you know where to find me," Bobby said, pulling the steel door open and stepping inside.

"'Sleep in my bed!'"

Four

ANSWERS IN THE ALLEY
Wednesday

The vibration of Relly's phone jolted in his pocket. Once again, the old-school quick piano jazz of Jelly Roll erupted across the rooftop. The early-morning sun slowly rose higher, causing the sky to turn yellowish orange. Relly pulled the phone out and ran his finger across the screen. Immediately, Monica's face popped up.

Monica smiled. Through the screen, Relly saw her yawn. With her free hand, she ran toothpaste across a toothbrush. Water rushed from a faucet.

"Sorry I couldn't text back. My abuelita made dinner last night, and after we ate, I was out"—Monica clicked two fingers together—"like that," she said, now brushing her teeth.

"It's cool," Relly said, standing up from the bench. He turned around and lifted the toe of his shoes against the base of the bench. Relly began to stretch his calves one at a time. Then Relly turned and began to pace. From the bench to the center of the rooftop and back.

"You're outside early," Monica said, now patting her face with a washcloth. "Show doesn't start till two."

"Came up to get some air. Then Bobby and I had a talk. I think something is wrong with me, Monica."

"I'm all ears. Always," Monica said as Relly heard a door close through the phone. "Tell me about it."

"Would you believe me if I told you I'm seeing things?" Relly reached the middle of the rooftop. Then he turned to face the bench. Instead of pacing, Relly paused. He stopped. His eyes narrowed, locking on to what he noticed underneath.

"Seeing things? What? I can't see your face. Say it again," Monica said. Relly held the phone up steady. "Hey! I had an idea," said Monica as Relly looked from the screen to the bench to the piece of wood underneath. Relly looked back to Monica.

"Slumber party at my house tonight. Abuelita makes the perfect sugar cookies, polvorones rosas, and Hudson keeps begging to try them."

"There's a piece of wood under the bench," he said, this

time walking closer. Relly had not noticed the wood on the rooftop floor the other times he had come up. Not even minutes earlier, when he and Bobby had talked.

"Also meant to tell you: Know what I tell my younger brother, Freddy, when he has something on his mind? When you hold inside what is bothering you, it'll grow into a volcano. Then it'll overflow like lava. Como una avalancha. Hold it in too long and it'll cool and crust over, like magma. We're friends, Relly. You know you can talk to me."

Relly heard Monica, but he did not respond as he walked closer to the bench. Then he stooped, still holding the phone in one hand. Relly lifted his arm and stretched.

"Hey, are you even listening?"

"I've been seeing visions, Monica," Relly said as he reached for the piece of wood.

"Visions? What kind of visions?" Monica asked. "Like a mirage?"

Relly reached and held the piece of wood between his thumb and index finger, as if it were a pencil. Looking down, this one was almost the same as the first piece he had found. Each edge was smooth and precise. When he flipped it over, there were waves of brown lines etched in the wood.

"Relly?"

Before Relly could respond, his fingertips began to tingle. Relly dropped the phone as the tingling inched up his right arm, then it traveled across his shoulders. Next, it inched down his left arm, before tingling across his shoulders again. The tingling turned to tickling. Relly let out a laugh. The tickling maneuvered down his spine, into his feet. Relly wiggled his toes. If Monica was still talking, Relly didn't hear her. He knew what came next. Blurred vision. The rooftop around him began to change. The rooftop blurred and morphed. Each edge of brick eased into a wavy line before straightening up into a single two-story building. On the building was a sign:

STANLEY BROWN DANCE STUDIO

One floor had a facade of brick. The top floor was made of three long, arched windows. But this moment didn't last as Relly gripped the piece of wood tighter. Soon, even the two-story building changed. Now Relly could see inside.

On the second floor, in the room with the arched windows, the light of the sun shone through. There were two people in this room. The first was a boy Relly's height, Relly's complexion, Relly's age. The second was a tall man giving instruction. Both the boy's and instructor's shadows reached from one end of the room to the opposite.

These were stretched out, elongated heel-and-toe tapping shadows. Feet-shuffling shadows. Toe-standing shadows. Then the shadow of the boy slid. It was a glide, an exact match to the man who Relly had seen at the bodega. The man in his first vision. Next, Relly heard the instructor clap.

"You're a bona fide expert. Quick learner. Kiddo, call yourself Slyde!" the instructor said. The boy looked up and smiled.

Relly dropped the sliver of tree before falling to his knees. As he let his eyes adjust, the rooftop came back. Relly looked for his phone.

"Monica! You there? Did you see that?" Relly asked, reaching for the device. But when he picked it up, Monica wasn't there. The screen was back to apps and icons. *Call ended* had popped up at the top. Relly swiped up and pressed to redial Monica's number. He waited, listening to the rings, but there was no answer.

Relly knew, downstairs, Grandpa and Momma would be waking up to start their day. Bobby would be wondering why Relly wasn't down to help with breakfast. Even though it was still early, Relly needed his own time to get ready for the Wednesday matinee show. Relly would have to catch up with Monica later.

During the two o'clock matinee, the lights on stage were bright. Relly could never tell how many people took up seats, but he could always feel a full audience. At the end of his own number, when the Squad jumped barrel after barrel, not a single laugh went unnoticed. At the end of each act, every single applause was felt. And the moisture from the waterfall scene that always landed on those sitting in the orchestra seats, Relly could hear every shock, each gasp. Every single awe. Clearly, trying new moves Tuesday had not caused a stir with *Our Time* fans.

But what Relly did notice were the eyes. The eyes of each cast member, not just April, Monica, and Hudson. Eyes from ensemble and the adult actors. Then there were eyes from the crew. Stagehands standing in the wings, watching. But the pair of eyes that caught Relly's attention the most, the pair that caused the tip of his spine to prickle, was from Claudia Middleton.

Relly felt as if he were a specimen on the wrong side of a magnifying glass. When the show was over, after the bows and hugs of yet another show complete, Claudia Middleton did not say a word. She only scribbled on a new page in her tiny notebook and left backstage before Relly could even walk past.

After the show, the Squad gathered in Relly and Hudson's dressing room. Music ripped from April's phone. Monica sat in a chair kicking her feet back and forth. She had made no mention of what had happened on the rooftop.

"Added. Added. Added," April said each time she added a new follower. "Oh, you're adding me? Sure," she said each time a new follower added her. "You've got to give your followers what they want. You know what I asked my followers on Insta the other day? 'What content do you want to see from me?' You know what my followers messaged back?"

"Tell us, April. We're jumping up and down dying to know." Hudson made his voice monotone. Relly didn't think a single one of them had any interest in what her followers messaged.

"'Give more secrets.' The people want the secrets! 'Tell us Broadways secrets!'" As April checked for more tagged posts, Hudson held out another box of goodies. For the past twenty minutes, he had tried to convince Monica to take them to her abuelita.

"Your grandma will love these!" Hudson exclaimed, showing Monica a tin of freshly baked praline cookies. "My grandma says they taste exactly like the ones her grandma used to make. Family recipe. It's been passed down for generations. Three, to be exact."

"She told me last night she's still working on those you gave her three days ago." Monica laughed. "Which reminds me: I told Relly earlier we should have a sleepover. Slumber party at my house tonight, and Abuelita can show you how to make the best cookies."

"Ooh! I like that idea! Hudson, know what else you should do? You could start a club! You know, for the grandmas. It could be a cookie club," April said without looking up from her phone. "You could put them on your FoodTube. The grandmas will be a hit!" Relly couldn't tell if April was joking or not.

"Speaking of FoodTube, guess who's starring in an episode this weekend."

"Who?" Relly, April, and Monica asked. Since Hudson's virtual cooking show had taken off, Relly knew it could have been any celebrity making a guest appearance.

"Selena Gomez."

"Selena Gomez!" April exclaimed. "Forget the cookies, let's go to Al Joseph's for food. This calls for a celebration. *The* Selena Gomez, Hudson? *The* Selena Gomez! Oh, can I come? Please? Can I be the second special guest?" April stopped her music. "Don't you think Selena Gomez would just love me? Ooh! Let me see check her Insta."

"You think we can get a table?" Relly asked. "It's late notice." He could use food. The Squad was always hungry after the show, so it seemed like the right call.

"Slumber party at Monica's after Al Joseph's! Tell your parents, kids!" April said, already sending her parents texts. "And, Relly, of course we can get a table." April started out the dressing-room door. "Don't you know they know who we are? And if they don't, they are about to find out." The Squad gathered up their belongings. Relly watched Hudson and Monica send quick texts. He grabbed his backpack, still making sure it was closed tight. Then Relly pulled out his phone to text Bobby.

R: Slumber party @ Monica's tonight. See u in the AM.

B: . . . Momma says if Monica's abuelita cooks, she wants a plate.

R: K.

B: Whatevs.

Then he followed the Squad out of the dressing room and down the hall.

"Al Joseph's, huh?" Jimmy said as he let the Squad exit the stage door.

"How'd you know?" Hudson asked.

"Listen, kids, I know the look of a hungry cast. I know what all that jumpin' and kickin' and slidin'"—Jimmy looked to Relly—"does to ya. That look, yous four got it."

The Squad stepped outside as some lingering fans let out a squeal. April, Monica, and Hudson promptly begun to sign autographs. Even if they wanted to dip out, there were always a few fans standing and waiting for the cast to come outside.

"I'll meet you at Al Joseph's!" Relly hollered out to his friends. He had a question for Jimmy. One that needed answers now. As Jimmy kept the stage door open, Relly gave Monica a concerned look. Relly needed to ask Monica a question too. Did she see the vision he had had on the rooftop? And why did the phone end the call? But he only mouthed *See you soon* as he stepped back inside the Ethel Merman Theater.

When the door closed, the stage-door doorman picked up the newspaper from his table, took a seat, and started to read. He hummed a tune vaguely like a Frank Sinatra song. Relly found himself pacing.

"Let it out, kid," Jimmy said, tapping his fingers to the table. "If there's something on your mind that bad, no sense holding it all in."

"What did you mean last night?"

"You will have to be more specific."

"You asked if something got me rattled. You said you know the look of an actor startled. You said if I want to talk, I know where to find you."

"That what I said?"

"That's what I heard."

When Jimmy didn't say anything else, Relly started to pace. This time frantic, until he stopped and picked up a pencil from the table. He moved it from each finger on his left hand. Then he grabbed the pencil with his right hand and did the same. Relly eyed the magic tricks and joke books in the cubbies above Jimmy's table. Over and over, the pencil twirled, until Relly finally let it all out.

"I saw something strange yesterday. Saw something

strange today, too." Relly felt a tickle of guilt for telling Jimmy before he told the Squad.

"Did you, now? In this city, we see things every day, kid. I've lost count of all the unexplainable, inexplicable things I've seen. You know how many people have come to my stage doors? Not only this one at the Ethel Merman. All of 'em. You won't believe the tales folks have told me."

Relly shook his head. "No, Jimmy! You don't understand. What I mean is, I saw a vision, only it was alive. It was real. There was this man tapping at the bodega, but how he glided across the stage, I've never seen anyone move like that in my life. And this morning, I saw a kid learning how to tap. Only it was at a dance studio on my rooftop!"

"A dancing man at a bodega, huh?"

"Jimmy! I cannot stop thinking about him. During the show Monday night, I didn't mean to try a new move; it came to me. It was that man's move. I felt it in my bones. I felt it so much, I couldn't stop. I couldn't help myself. And now my grandpa is making me think I should find a backup plan."

"Who is he? Give me a name. Give me a description. Give me some type of clue."

"My grandpa?"

"The bodega man."

"I. Do. Not. Know!" Relly tapped out each word. "And

Claudia thinks I'm in a weird slump. And Monica probably thinks I hung up on her! What is happening to me? Jimmy, everybody thinks I've been off. Relly Morton is never off!"

"Did you just refer to yourself in third person?" Jimmy sighed as he stood, pulling the stage door open again.

"You don't believe me? See, I knew no one would believe me. Which means April, Monica, and Hudson won't believe me either. Do you think it's the curse again? Could it have come back? Is it making me see things?" Relly asked as he walked toward the open door.

"Curses you know. Conundrums you don't."

"What does that even mean?" Relly shouted in frustration.

"It means there are answers in the alley, Relly. Answers are always present where history has taken place."

"I thought you said come to you to talk, not hear a riddle," Relly said. Jimmy stood outside the door as he let Relly exit.

"I said you could come to me, and you did, didn't you?"

Before Relly could prod Jimmy with more questions, the stage door shut. Relly felt as if he were in the same spot from ten minutes ago. And still no answers. But Relly would have to take Jimmy's response as some sort of solution.

Or clue.

Relly turned on his heels and ran. Out the door, past the Ethel, down the street. His heart thumped as his feet pushed off against the ground. Relly shook out both hands, as if the movement would loosen the frazzled feeling inside. His phone vibrated and the Jelly Roll piano jazz ringtone went off in his pocket. When the phone chimed, Relly jumped, almost bumping into a family of tourists snapping a picture. He ran until it felt like his feet weren't hitting the pavement at all. Relly pulled out his phone, keeping one eye on the sidewalk, one eye on the screen. Both feet in forward motion.

Hudson: Relly! Dude! Where are you?!!?

April: OMG. We got the best table! Hurry up 4 a pic!

Monica: You coming?

Hudson: More food 4 me if u don't.

April: Selena Gomez!

Relly tapped his phone. He frantically typed with shaky fingers.

Relly: Meet me in the alley. We can eat later!

Relly turned down Shubert Alley. The narrow path stretched between several different theaters with rows of show posters. *Aladdin* and *Memphis*! *Come from Away* and *Wicked*! The show poster for *Our Time* was in the middle of all the others. Pax, Crash, Tony, and Froggie were frozen in motion on the tall poster. Relly stopped. He couldn't help but look at his reflection in the *Our Time* poster. Relly tilted his head at the image. Finally, he caught his breath.

You always have two choices: your commitment ver-

sus your fear. Relly remembered a Sammy Davis Jr. quote Momma used to say. Then he took a step back, but the rough pavement of the alley made him do a kind of half step. Relly was not one to trip or stumble, always nimble and smooth on his feet. But for the past day, "smooth" and "nimble" were not words he would use to describe himself.

"Ah!" Relly caught his footing before hitting the pavement. He breathed a sigh of relief. But he only caught himself because he tripped into someone. When he turned around, it was April.

"We were about to or—aaah!" April said as she tripped over the same dip in the pavement. One second her phone was in her hand, then it was midair. April grasped for her phone but missed. Her shoulder nudged into Monica's arm. Monica's arm collided with Hudson's and his tray of cookies, which scattered all over the sidewalk.

"My phone!" April hollered. Her voice bounced off the Shubert and Booth theaters. It swung off the show posters attached to their walls: *Hamilton*; *In the Heights*; *Natasha, Pierre & the Great Comet of 1812*! April's shout of "My phone!" cascaded between buildings. Relly stood, wide-eyed and opened-mouthed. He, Monica, and Hudson watched as the cell phone plummeted straight into a sewer. "This cannot be happening."

It was happening.

Five

"Are you serious?" This time April's words were barely over a whisper. "We left Al Joseph's for this? How am I supposed to give my followers updates? My mom is going to flip. I can't tell her I lost my phone. She'll say I exhibit lack of responsibility. She'll ban me from technology for life. She's been telling me to take a hiatus from social media, and it looks like she got her wish."

There was a distinct *plop, pling-clang*. Then nothing. The phone had clearly settled into the depths below.

Relly pointed out the obvious: "You know, your phone isn't lost."

"Yeah, I mean, we know exactly where it is." Hudson

nodded toward the hole. He frowned at his scattered treats on the alley sidewalk.

"I'll get it." Relly stooped to peer inside. The frazzled feeling Relly had when he left the Ethel Merman Theater crept up in his throat. There would be no phone in a sewer if Relly hadn't asked his friends to meet him in the alley. Down below looked inklike and gloomy. But before his friends could object, Relly stepped down. He secured his hands around the edges of the opening and his feet on the ladder rungs below.

"You don't have to do that, Relly," said Monica. "April, phones can be replaced."

"Eh, it's just a drain." he said. He didn't wait for April's reply before descending into the shadowy, unlit depth. *It's just a drain, right?*

One leg, then the other, Relly plunged into the manhole. One foot, then the next pressed off the old rusty ladder rungs. Each one wobblier than the last. When Relly's hands touched each rung, they felt cold with wet slime.

Relly's stomach churned. The farther down he stepped into the shadows, the more his nose took in a scent worse than every single dumpster in New York City. Worse than the time Bobby attempted to cook dinner and used two-week-old milk in the mac and cheese. The smell reeked. What did not help was that the farther Relly stepped into the depths, the more he had a feeling he was not supposed to be there. April's frantic words from above traveled down the manhole and bounced off each ladder rung.

"What if it's broken? What if my screen's cracked? Please, please don't let my phone get wet."

"What happens if your phone gets wet?" Relly heard Hudson ask. His words sounded muffled too.

"Pictures. Videos. Gone."

"Forget your phone, April," Monica said. "Relly, are you okay?" she yelled into the hole. Relly climbed down faster.

"Yeah!" he hollered. "So far, so great." Until his feet hit concrete. They splashed into a puddle of thick, murky water.

"Oh, that's disgusting."

Relly pulled out his own phone and swiped up to the flashlight. He tilted the phone left, then right, holding it up as far as it would go. The light spread on the wet walls.

"Find anything?" Hudson hollered from above. "Or are you still climbing?"

"No and no!" Relly hollered back. He lifted his phone, letting the flashlight illuminate the path ahead. One long tunnel stretched. There was no exit in sight.

"Don't see it! I'm going to walk a little deeper."

"If it went straight down, it can't be far!" April yelled. That's exactly what Relly hoped.

When his foot hit something solid, it gently slid the

object out of the way. But the solid object felt familiar. Relly hovered his phone over his shoes and saw a purple phone case, facedown. Lucky for April, it wasn't in water. It didn't even look wet. The purple phone with the image of Aladdin's genie wasn't even damp. The genie held up the golden lamp.

"Found it!" Relly yelled. "You guys!" He hoped they could hear. "April, I found your phone!" An eruption of cheers poured into the tunnel. "And it's not even wet!"

"It keeps getting better!" Relly heard April yell.

"All right, I'm coming back up," Relly shouted, tapping April's phone. He swiped up and turned on its flashlight. Now he had double the light. Relly lit the path ahead. The two phone flashlights lit up the concrete walls. Only, these walls ahead were dry with show posters. Broadway show posters were fastened to the wall in a neat and orderly sequence. Exactly like the ones above in Shubert Alley. But these below were faded.

"What is all this?" Relly muttered. He walked past each one, lifting both phones so their flashlights hovered over each poster.

There was *A Raisin in the Sun*, the Lorraine Hansberry play. One of Momma's favorites. Then there was a poster from *West Side Story*. Relly could make out a line that said, *A New Musical!* Then there was *The Music Man*, and a faded green-and-white poster from *Peter Pan*.

What stood out to Relly most were spray-painted words sprinkled between the posters. Faded graffiti graced the walls.

Keep going!

A little farther.

You can do it!

Up from here!

"You guys! YOU HAVE GOT TO COME SEE THIS!"

After several minutes of silence, Relly was relieved when the Squad finally found him. Hudson made up the back of the group, reluctant to inch farther into the damp sewer. But when they reached Relly, they, too, stood in front of the posters and graffiti in a type of confused shock.

"All this down here? What is this place?" Hudson asked. "How'd it get here?"

Relly shrugged. *How would I know?* He had been trying to figure out how, or why, anyone would place show posters and graffiti in a sewer.

"Are they all from the same time?" asked Monica.

"The same decade. The 1950s."

"These are ancient." April grabbed her phone from Relly. "May as well have been a century ago. My mom used to tell me that her mom told her the fifties were the golden years. Can you imagine living with no modern technology? No cell phones. No internet. No social media. Black-and-white television. And the food, eek! Why did they put Jell-O in everything? I can't. I cannot. I would lose my mind. I mean, imagine the boredom. Imagine the lack of taste."

"Shh," Relly whispered as he nodded to a closed steel door. It stood shut, ten feet ahead. Relly's cell phone flashlight shone on the door. It cast an eerie light on the silver steel.

"I'm looking for answers," Relly whispered. "Jimmy said they would be here."

"Answers to what? Relly, what's wrong with you? What's up?" Hudson's voice cracked as he asked each question.

"That's what I'm trying to find out."

"You need answers? Simple: use Google. It's an answer encyclopedia."

Relly ignored Hudson as he touched his hand to the cool doorknob. He gripped the knob tight. His heart felt like it was on top of his tonsils. A drop of sweat dripped off the brim of his nose, but Relly still twisted the knob and pushed. April, Monica, and Hudson held their breath until Relly got the door open. On the other side was a ladder. The Squad exhaled.

"A ladder!" Relly said.

"A ladder?" asked Monica.

"Such a letdown," April commented.

Relly began to climb. He was followed by April, who was followed by Monica. They were followed by Hudson, who figured he had no other choice. Relly's hand felt the heavy, round cover up above. He slipped his fingers through the holes and pleaded that a car or person would not trample over his digits. He needed his feet to dance, and he needed his fingers, too.

Then Relly pushed. Up and over, he slid the cover to the left. Then he peeked over the edge of the opening in the middle of what was clearly Shubert Alley. Only this was not the Shubert Alley the Squad had left ten minutes ago.

"Come on, Relly," Hudson said down below. "Hurry up, please! We can't move any farther!"

Relly took the remaining ladder rungs slow. He calculated his steps, careful that his sneakers might make him slip. Once Relly's feet reached the top of the opening, he looked up and saw light flicks of clouds that dotted the sky. Altocumulus. Relly remembered the type from the time Amanda, the Squad's tutor, had taught a lesson on meteorology.

"Expect a thunderstorm when you see those bad boys! Expect a change in the weather!" Amanda said inside their classroom at the Ethel one afternoon. Change. The sky above Shubert Alley before they walked through the sewer was blue and clear. There was not a single cloud in sight before they entered the sewer. Now this sky was different.

As Relly reached up out the hole in the ground and stepped up onto the pavement, his friends scrambled out of the hole behind him. Up aboveground, the air was fresh and crisp. A swift wind hit Relly and coated his skin with warmth. It had to have been ten degrees warmer now than when they first entered the sewer. At that moment, Relly knew they had stepped straight into the word Jimmy had used back at the Ethel Merman. "Conundrum." Even the shade of blue in the sky was much lighter than what they had left behind.

"What time is it?" Relly asked. April pulled her phone from her pocket and gave the home screen three quick taps. She shook the phone vigorously, gripping both sides tight in one hand. April pressed the power button.

"It's not doing anything. It's not even turning on. Why is my phone not turning on? My phone never not turns on. Are you sure it didn't get wet, Relly?" April's words were frantic. "It was on eighty percent ten minutes ago. I have a brand-new battery. I barely keep it off the charger. Relly, my phone never not works! You know why my phone never not works? Because I keep it updated. You know why I keep it updated? Because my phone always works! Why is my phone not working!"

The rest of the Squad pulled their phones out too. Relly tapped his home screen. He pressed the power button. The device was blank.

"Nothing," said Monica, confused. "I can't even check if I have service."

"Yep, mine's dead," said Hudson. When Relly looked back at April, she was still staring at her screen, shocked and blank-faced until she let out a shriek. The shriek was the sign of someone who never went five minutes without posting a new story or making a new TikTok.

"There has to be some type of explanation," Monica began. "Maybe the moisture in the sewer got to our phones?"

"Or the smell," said Hudson.

Relly didn't have an answer either. Because besides their phones being dead, this Shubert Alley was . . . off. The marquees above each theater's doors were not digital like the ones they had just left. They did not scroll and flash in multicolored lights. They did not blink any Broadway show's name. Instead, the marquees were plain, only stating the name of the musicals and plays in bold, curvy letters. DINOSAUR WHARF. HAMLET. THE WILD DUCK. TWELFTH NIGHT. REMAINS TO BE SEEN.

"I have never seen some of these shows before," said Relly. Besides the Shakespeare plays, the rest of the Squad had not heard of the other shows either. They were not the current shows on Broadway.

Here, there were no show posters from *Our Time* or *Wicked, Aladdin* or *Hamilton.* Relly looked to the people who walked up and down the alley. The people here were dressed different, too. There was a woman in a floral dress with a fanned-out skirt. She wore triangle glass frames on her face. On top of her head was the thinnest, tiniest hat Relly had ever seen. The woman took long, elegant strides as she rushed past. Then, going the opposite direction, was a family of four dressed in their best. Lace-trimmed gloves, lace-trimmed dresses, patent-leather shoes. The mother, father, and two children also rushed up the alley. Clearly, they were on their way to see a show.

"Can they see us?" asked Hudson. "Or . . . is this the other side? I didn't see a light in that tunnel. Did you all see a light?! Are we . . . *dead*?"

"Don't be ridiculous," said Relly, still taking in the scene. No, they were not dead. From the way his heart thumped at the difference in this Shubert Alley, they were each very much alive. And when a light blue Cadillac with rolled-down windows drove past the Shubert Alley entrance, Relly's ears took in the music coming from the car's radio.

Go, Johnny, go! Go! Go, Johnny, go! Go! Johnny B. Goode.

"Cute lyrics, but that's on old song," said April, still trying to turn on her phone.

"It's a Chuck Berry song," said Relly.

"How do you know Chuck Berry?" asked Hudson.

"My mom. She plays all the old-school music from her radio."

Six

12:00 P.M.

Eight hours until Our Time

By now Relly had noticed a boy across the street leaning against the side of a *Peter Pan* poster. In the green, white, and gray poster, Peter flew in front of a background of stars. Both hands were stretched out, and on his face was an equally stretched smile. He was the only one in the alley, besides the Squad, not in a rush to get somewhere.

The boy wore suspenders connected with silver clasps attached to brown pants. On his feet were thick black shoes. Relly's grandfather used to call those types of shoes loafers. Relly had noticed the boy because the boy was staring dead at Relly. Eyes locked, like Relly was a magnet.

The kid had to be no more than eight. No more than a few years younger than Relly.

"Has he been looking at us the whole time?" Relly asked, nodding his head toward the kid. April, Hudson, and Monica turned to look.

"You think he saw us come out the sewer and all? You think he can see us? Relly, you think he knows we're dead?"

"Hudson! We are not dead." Relly pointed to the kid. "He can see us all right." Relly began to walk across the alley, ignoring Hudson's exaggerated panic.

"What are you doing?!"

Relly maneuvered between people until he finally reached the boy.

"Um, hi, hello there," Relly said as he approached. He waved, but the boy stood there and stared. Relly only wanted to ask the kid a question. "Can you tell me what time it is?"

For a moment, the kid opened his mouth, then closed it shut. He opened his mouth again, hesitating before he said, "Noon." The boy's words came out quieter than Relly expected.

"Noon? What do you mean it's noon? It was almost five in the evening ten minutes ago!"

"Well, that's the time my watch is telling me." The boy looked down at a silver watch around his wrist. "See?" He held the wristwatch up for Relly to see. Relly took one more glance around at the out-of-date posters. A nearby advertisement showed Pepsi-Cola in a glass bottle. The words "peachy keen" were written in bold red letters.

"What's today?"

"Huh? What's it to you? What kind of question is that?"

"The day, please! What's the day?" Relly pleaded.

"March sixth, duh. Last time I checked my dad's calendar, which was ten this morning, it was Thursday, March sixth."

"The year?" Relly asked. "What's the year!" he repeated, more frantic the longer it took the kid to answer.

"1958. Year of the dog. Everybody knows that."

Relly's throat tightened. His palms got slick with sweat. Relly forgot to say thank you as he ran back to his friends. Because, how? *How?* It was not March 6 when they entered the alley. It was not Thursday when they walked through the sewer. And it for sure was not anywhere near noon. Yet somehow, now that they were up and out of the sewer, it was March 6, Thursday, at noon. Nineteen fifty—what?

"Put your phones away!" Relly shouted as he ran back to his friends. He unzipped his backpack, which had the two pieces of wood, and dropped his phone inside. Then Relly held the backpack open for the others to do the same. "Put them in here."

"Why?" April asked as Hudson and Monica dropped theirs in. "They aren't working anyway."

"Why? Let me tell you why. It's March sixth! Which means it's Thursday! Which means it's 1958! Which means it is noon, and that means we only have eight hours until *Our Time*. You hear me? Eight hours! I can't be late. Grandpa Gregory is coming to see the show. Why? Cause it's his birthday. Why is it his birthday? Because this is the day he was born! Please tell me why we're in the past and what is going on!" Relly held his breath. He wasn't sure if that would help him catch it, but it was worth a try. When Relly released, the air in his mouth whooshed out. He zipped up his backpack with their phones inside as sweat poured down his face.

"Calm down. Calm down," Hudson said. Relly didn't understand why Hudson wasn't panicking too. Wasn't Hudson *just* panicking?

"Don't tell me to calm down."

"But, Relly, isn't the real question 'How did we get here?' Am I right? Am I correct?" Hudson laughed, thinking he made a funny. His words were not hilarious to Relly.

"No. The real question is, 'How do we get home?'" April said. "Present-day home. Gimme my phone. I'm gonna try to call my mom."

"No! April"—Relly pulled his backpack around his

shoulders—"our phones aren't working. Plus, I've seen one too many time-travel movies. You know what happens if we mess with the timeline? You know what happens if we put even one thing out of place?"

"Our future gets negated," said Monica, alarmed.

"What's that mean?" asked Hudson.

"It means our future gets messed up."

"All the way messed up. Which means we might make ourselves not exist and that means we cannot use our phones," said Relly. "Somehow, time jumped. When we entered the hole, it was Wednesday. When we exited, it's almost a whole day later, Thursday, at noon. The tunnel must have been some sort of portal. Some kind of time machine." At least that's what Relly thought. Then Relly thought back to how they ended up in the alley in the first place.

"Jimmy."

"What's Jimmy have to do with this?" asked Monica.

"Oh no. I'm going back. I'm going back! No way am I going to be stuck in the fifties. I was not made for a time other than my own! What about my cooking show, Relly? I have another batch of cookies to make—brownie-flavored cookies! How am I supposed to film my episode of *Broadway Sizzlers* with *the* one and only Selena Gomez if I am stuck in 1958?"

Hudson hurried over to the sewer hole. But when he

got there and knelt to climb down, the cover had been slid back. Hudson tried to pull the cover up. Yet, the more he pulled, the more it would not budge. Hudson tried lifting and tugging and heaving and yanking. No matter how much he yanked and tugged and tried to lift, the steel cover may as well have been superglued shut.

Relly watched as Hudson put his fingers through the holes in the cover. Relly continued to watch as Hudson squeezed his fingers between the holes like claws. Then Hudson began to shake. The round steel cover did nothing. It did not move. When Hudson had enough of his efforts not working, Relly watched as he picked up what Relly thought was a piece of trash. Hudson held it in one hand, on the verge of tossing it in frustration. It seemed the piece of trash was a stretched baseball and Hudson's hand was a Louisville Slugger. Then Relly saw it was not trash at all.

"Wait! Wait. Where did you get this?" Relly asked, grabbing what Hudson held in his hand. It was another thick sliver of brown wood. Like the one from the bodega and the one from the rooftop.

"It was next to that!" Hudson said, pointing down at the manhole cover. "The thing that won't move so we can get back home!"

"Didn't you say you found wood on the rooftop when we FaceTimed?" Monica asked.

Relly held the piece of wood closer. It matched the two others in his backpack. Now, with the third piece of wood in Relly's hands, it didn't take long for the tingling and blurry vision to happen. The feeling flowed over Relly as he closed his eyes. Not knowing what he would see this time, Relly kept his eyes shut. The feeling reminded him of the feeling he had every Christmas morning. The feeling of having a gift wrapped in fancy paper in the palm of his hands. The feeling of there being an unknown surprise inside.

Relly opened his eyes to a new scene. It was the sight of a momma and child sitting at a dining room. This momma reminded Relly of his momma, with a pink-and-yellow floral silk scarf tied across her head. Thick curls cascaded from the sides and over the top. The child at the table was much younger than the first two visions Relly had seen. The child was no more than nine, and in his hands was a violin.

"You play so well, Gregory," the momma said. "My little music man. Don't you want to play music instead of tap?" Relly saw the boy place the violin and its bow on the table. The boy stood. He shook his head. He moved his feet. He tapped his toes against the floor.

"I don't want to play music. I want to dance music," he told his mother as he patted his feet against the floor.

"Dance music? And why is that?" the momma asked.

"Because when I dance, I fly," the boy said.

Relly sucked in his breath. "Me too," Relly whispered, dropping the piece of wood. The vision dissolved. Quickly, Shubert Alley and the Squad were back.

"What just happened?" April's voice shook. "You looked like you saw a ghost. Did you see a ghost? Did you even hear us call your name? I've never seen anyone so still before in my life. That's a long time, 'cause I'm almost thirteen! Were you in a trance? Monica, didn't he look like he was in a trance?"

"Is this what happened on the rooftop, Relly? I saw you freeze, then the phone went dead!"

"I think they are clues," Relly whispered as he gasped for air. He stared down at the piece of wood on the ground.

"W-would someone please tell me what's going on!" Hudson stammered. "First we go through a sewer. Then we end up in the fifties. Now you're seeing things? Do you need some water or . . ." Hudson looked at the billboard advertisement. "Pepsi-Cola?"

"Whatever these are," Relly began, tapping the piece of wood with his foot, "they make me see things. And nope, I don't need water or Pepsi-Cola." Hudson raised an eyebrow.

"I need to tell you what happened to me. I need to tell you about the bodega."

Seven

1:00 P.M.

Seven hours until Our Time

The only reason Hudson, Monica, and April were stuck in the past was because Relly had led them there. He had to tell the Squad why he had been late for Tuesday's show. It was time he let them know why he had seemed "off" and frazzled and flustered.

Before he began, Relly crossed his fingers. He uncrossed them, then crossed his toes. Monica tapped Relly on his arm.

"Hey, you've got this," Monica said.

Relly started with Momma asking him and Bobby to pick up ingredients for the cake. Then, his walking dance, dancing walk to the bodega. Then, Nita making his brother a sandwich. Next, Relly recalled how he leapt up and down aisle three.

"I did precisely three fouettés," Relly said, trying to remember. "Maybe four, but no more than five!"

This piece of information was followed by picking up the rest of the pineapples for his grandfather's cake. "Pineapple upside-down." Then Relly recounted how he saw a piece of wood on the shelf.

"I thought she was selling timber!"

He told them in as much detail about how the bodega transformed when he touched the piece of wood. How it felt when he saw the bodega morph. Everything from the theater with its chandelier to the clothing in which people were dressed to the man who danced on stage. *Especially the man who danced on stage.* He was the same one from the two other visions, only in those the man was younger.

"What about the rooftop?" Monica asked. "Remember, when we were on the phone, you said something was under the bench. Then I saw you walk forward, but I couldn't see your face. Next thing I knew, you stooped down, but the phone went blank."

"I found a piece of wood on my building rooftop, too. It was under the bench with my dad's name. And when I touched it, my arms started to tingle. In that vision, I saw a kid learning how to tap from a choreographer. At some dance studio I've never heard of."

"What about the wood from the sewer?" Hudson asked, pointing to the sewer cover. "What about what just happened to you?"

"Looked like you were in a daze," April said.

"It was another vision!" Relly said. "And in that one, the kid was a little younger than me. He was with his mom. The kid told her he wanted to tap."

The Squad nodded and listened, quiet as Relly talked. They let him get his words out without a single interruption. Relly knew this was almost impossible for April. After Relly finished the story, there was a pause as if the Squad was waiting to hear more. He didn't have more to add. When they realized Relly's story was finished, Monica was the first to nod. Then Hudson followed, next came April. It was a nod of understanding. And even though Relly thought they wouldn't believe him, he was shocked when they did.

"What I don't understand is where the pieces of wood came from. Why am I the one to find them? Who is the man in the visions? What's it all mean?"

Monica gave Relly a sympathetic smile.

"I'm sorry about all this, Relly," Monica said. "Ni en mis sueños más locos lo imaginé, not even in my craziest dreams could I imagine. That's what Abuelita always tells me. Wish we knew how to help. I wish we knew exactly what to do."

"Um, yeah," Hudson said low, raising his eyebrows. "Now that I think about it, being stuck in nineteen fifty-eight is nothing compared to what you've been through. Jeez."

Relly wasn't sure he believed Hudson's words. Even he wasn't happy to be stuck in the fifties. But when Monica, April, and Hudson took a few steps forward and wrapped Relly in a group hug, he felt an inch of relief.

They believed me! Relly thought.

"I'm sorry; it's my fault we're stuck here right now." When Relly looked up, his eyes darted to the boy still staring from the *Peter Pan* poster. "It's my fault we're in the fifties."

"Don't blame yourself. It's not like you knew we would end up here," said Hudson.

"Can I see?" April asked, holding out her hand. "I kind of want to know what it's like to see a vision. Come on, Relly, hurry! We can't stand here all day."

"I'm warning you." Relly lifted one piece of the wood. "Imagine being in one of those simulation roller coasters, except you don't remember ever stepping on."

"Can't be worse than me not being able to use my cell phone."

Relly hesitated, then passed the sliver of tree to April.

She reached out and grabbed it. She lifted it up and down in her hand. She flipped it over once, then over once more. Nothing happened. Not like it did for Relly. The sliver of wood was just that: lumber.

"What do you think it's for? I mean, it has purpose, right? It clearly does something to *you*. Here, Hudson, hold it." April tossed it to Hudson, who clumsily caught the piece of wood. Again, nothing happened. Hudson passed it to Monica. Nothing. Finally, Monica passed it back to Relly, who held his backpack open and let her drop it inside.

"It's you who sees these—what's it? Visions? Relly, maybe they are like clues," Monica said.

"Clues? I kind of thought about that before."

"Yep! Pieces to a puzzle."

"To finding out who the man in my visons is."

"It's the best lead we've come up with so far. Well, it's the only lead, for that matter," said Monica.

Relly pulled out the notebook he kept in his backpack. It brushed up against the pieces of wood. Then Relly jotted down the word "clues." Then he wrote the numbers one, two, and three. Relly wrote details of the three visions.

"This is all lovely, guys. Really, it is. Wonderful. Brilliant. Spectacular. We were literally blasted to the past. Such fun. Look. I want to know, and I hope you want to know, how the heck do we get home? Present-day home, where we have service and people don't dress like they walked out of *I Love Lucy*."

"*I Love Lucy!*" Hudson shouted. At those words, Hudson was the most excited Relly had seen him since they arrived in the fifties. "I love that old show, April."

April rolled her eyes. "So do I, but I don't exactly want to be in it."

"I want to get home too," Relly said. He didn't want to be stuck any more than his friends. "I can't be late for our show tonight. Claudia made that clear. Plus, my grandfather is seeing the show. Can you imagine what he'll say if Jacob performs and not me? He's already trying to get me to think about a backup plan."

"What kind of backup plan?" Hudson asked.

"Engineering workshops."

"Engineering? I mean, I know you like to fix things, but . . . that's not you," April said.

"Tell that to my grandpa, April."

"I think I know." Monica jumped. Her eyes watered in excitement. "Ooh, I have an idea, and it starts with Ethel."

"Ethel?" Relly asked. "Our Ethel?"

"Yep, the Ethel Merman. What if we find a show she was in? One from this decade. One from this year. Then we can ask Ethel to help us."

"How would she know how to get us home?" said

Hudson. "She would just be an ordinary celebrity living in the fifties."

"True. Good point. Touché," April said.

Relly remembered the show posters he had seen lined up along the sewer wall. He tried to recall what they looked like. There were so many. Even though he had light from his phone, it was dark inside that sewer. He couldn't take all of the posters in.

"True, Hudson. But I wouldn't call Ethel ordinary. More like an extraordinary celebrity in the fifties. And Ethel is legendary. Mythical. Her voice, for instance, unmatched. And all the weird stuff that happens inside the Ethel Merman Theater . . . sobrenatural. I say she knows something we don't," said Monica.

"*Gypsy*," said April. "That's one I saw. It looked like Ethel Merman on the poster. Let me tell you, by now I think I would recognize our Ethel anywhere."

"If we ask her for help, is that changing the timeline?" asked Relly.

"You asked that kid the time. I don't think it'll hurt anything," said Monica.

Hudson huffed. He looked to the sewer opening, then back to his friends. Relly knew Hudson wasn't about to climb back down, but it was clear Hudson was unconvinced.

"It's worth a try," said Relly.

The alley had gotten crowded since they had arrived in the fifties. A few moments ago, there had been only a few people walking up and down the path. Now there were dozens. A crowd had begun to gather. In the middle of Shubert Alley, they swarmed behind a velvet maroon rope barrier. In between the barricades was some type of red carpet. Person after person maneuvered down Shubert Alley. They stopped outside the stage door for the Booth theater.

"Ankle biters, always in the way." A man wearing suspenders said, squeezing past the Squad.

"What's an ankle biter?" April asked.

"I think it's fifties slang for 'child,'" said Monica.

"Child?"

"Technically, we are children."

Along the side of the building was a show poster that matched the one April had seen in the sewer. On it was a black-and-white image of Ethel Merman's smiling face. There were white-and-red letters that said the words:

GYPSY

A NEW MUSICAL!

In the poster, it looked like Ethel belted out a tune.

"Tell me I'm dreaming," said April. "Could you imagine if my phone worked? I could take a picture and show it to Jimmy back at our theater. Bet he wouldn't even believe me!"

"Welp, too bad you have no phone." At Hudson's words, the stage door swung open. The crowd silenced as a woman dressed in a purple sleeveless ball gown stepped out.

Ethel Merman.

In the flesh.

With each step, the crowd didn't budge. Not even a pigeon dared coo around Ethel. It was so mesmerizingly quiet. Relly thought if a feather were to fall from the sky, the entire captivated crowd would hear it.

In her ball gown, Ethel wore bold round pearl earrings. The tips of each fingernail were painted red. Ethel's brown hair was piled on top of her head, and each wisp of curl was held in perfect place. Ethel Merman embodied magnificence, elegance, an aura of exquisiteness. The live version of Ethel was a match to the statue of her that stood at the Ethel Merman Theater. Ethel was iconic and the statue was golden.

When Ethel walked the carpet, music followed. But Ethel was not singing. Ethel was not even speaking. Not yet. She only smiled with pen in hand as she began to sign autograph after autograph. *Playbill* after *Playbill*. Headshot after black-and-white headshot. The silence cascaded into a murmur. The murmur grew into a steady resonance. But the words weren't chatter. No. This murmur was from the crowd as they sang one of Ethel's songs.

"Pinch me!" Monica whispered. "I'm dreaming. I must be dreaming. Abuelita would trade places with me in a heartbeat. Oh, if she could be here right now!"

"There's no people like show people," Monica began to sing. April's voice joined in with Monica's. The voice of the singing crowd joined in with them both. Now the hundreds of people outside were singing. "This is our chance." Monica grabbed April's hand. "Let's take it." April squeezed Monica's hand tight. April then grabbed Relly's hand, and next, Relly grabbed Hudson's.

"So much for not messing with a timeline!" Hudson hollered. "What are we doing?"

"Finding a way home," Monica yelled behind her. "I hope!"

The four made a chain with their arms as they maneuvered between person after 1950s person. In and out they weaved. Relly shouted "Excuse me!" and "Coming through!" He knew that every few seconds his backpack was accidently knocking into someone. Finally, they reached the barricade.

"You cut the line!" someone yelled behind them. The crowd was clearly annoyed four kids—well, ankle biters— had jumped to the front. But now they stood only feet from Ethel Merman.

"Ethel!" Monica stood on tiptoes. "Ethel! Ethel!" She

attempted to get Ethel's attention. Monica waved at the Broadway turned Hollywood turned Broadway star. Then Ethel gave a slight lift of her eyebrow.

"How exactly is she supposed to help us?" Hudson asked Relly.

"Beats me."

Ethel stopped. She capped her pen and turned around. At least they had finally gotten Ethel's attention as she began to walk toward them. The crowd turned silent. All eyes were on Ethel. All eyes were on the Squad. All eyes waited to see what Ethel Merman would do, or say, or sing next. Then Ethel stopped directly in front of the Squad. Relly couldn't help but take in the legend. So poised. So elegant. So sure of herself. Relly didn't know if he would ever feel sure of himself again.

"I know who I am," Ethel declared.

There had been no performer like her, no performer who could match Ethel's originality. The Squad knew this, and Relly felt as much as all four took one simultaneous inhale. Then one lengthy exhale. Ethel lifted her hand to take a *Playbill*. But the Squad didn't have one. They didn't even have a headshot for Ethel to sign.

"We're a little empty-handed. We came here unprepared, right, Hudson?" Monica said.

"That's the understatement of this decade."

"But you can sign my arm!" April lifted her arm. Ethel Merman was not impressed.

"Actually, we're here because we think you can help us get home." Relly turned to Monica. "Should I tell her?" Monica nodded. Then Relly began to go into the spiel of how they found themselves in a sewer, then out of the sewer, into a place that seemed familiar but completely different at the same time. Ethel took in his words, silent until she turned to the teenage kid behind her.

"You hearing this, kid? They are telling me I have my own theater," Ethel said. "On Broadway. With a golden statue of moi! And that these four are Broadway stars stuck in a different decade? That should be a play in itself." Next, Ethel began to laugh. It was a belly laugh. It was a rowdy laugh. What's worse than Ethel Merman laughing? Ethel Merman laughing at you. What's worse than being laughed at by Ethel Merman? The entire crowd laughing too. "That's rich, kids!"

"This isn't working!" Relly turned to Monica. "We've got less than seven hours to get back before our next show, and she thinks we're lunatics," Relly said through his teeth as he glanced at the person behind Ethel, the slim teenage kid with black hair slicked back in the style of the decade. At first glance he was an ordinary teen clearly sent to give Ethel support. At second glance, when the kid took the green apple he was holding and bit into it, Relly knew he was Jimmy. The kid crunched and chewed, gulped then swallowed the bite of apple. Just like Jimmy did at the stage door. Yep, it was definitely a younger version of Jimmy.

"Jimmy Onions?" Relly asked.

"Jimmy Onions!" Hudson shouted.

"Jimmy!" Monica said as she placed her hands on the velvet-rope barrier. Jimmy nodded, then scrunched up his eyebrows.

"Do I know yous?" he asked before Ethel turned to young Jimmy and spoke so low, Relly could not hear her.

"Sorry! I'm in training and still learning parts of the job. Ethel says yous four are slowing up the line." The young Jimmy called to the *Our Time* cast. "Ethel says she doesn't have time to answer your endless questions."

"But we were . . . ," Monica started.

"Causing a disturbance. Yes." Ethel spoke. She turned to teenage Jimmy and whispered more.

"Ethel says it's time yous four leave," said young Jimmy.

"Leave?" Relly asked.

"Is that what he said?" asked Ethel.

"Yes!" the Squad responded.

"Okey doke, then that's what I meant!"

The crowd made a perfect path for the Squad to exit. As Ethel began to walk up the line, farther away from the

Squad, Relly knew their moment was over. So much for Monica's idea to get them home. It was a good try.

"That was a bust," said Hudson as they found themselves back in the same spot beside the closed sewer.

"You would think Jimmy would have at least tried to help."

"Yeah, but he has no clue who we are. And he's, what . . . looked about fifteen? Not like he has a time machine," said April.

"That much is true," Hudson said. "Listen. I don't know what we're going to do or how we're going to get home. What I do know is I'm hungry. You hear my belly? It's hungry. I'm in need of some food."

"Sounds like you're hangry to me."

"Hungry, hangry; April, it's all the same. I need sustenance. I can't think when my stomach wants food. Relly, do you think it'll be okay for us to grab a bite?" Hudson asked. "That won't mess up our present day, right? I won't have fifty fingers or something when we get back? Twenty toes? I'll still have my younger siblings, right?"

"Yeah." Relly shrugged. "I guess. I mean, food never hurt anybody, right? And we'll need all our brainpower to figure out how to get back. Food is a good call. Let's get a bite, but let's make it quick."

As the Squad walked up the alley, away from the sewer and the crowd, Relly looked behind him. He had a feeling they were being followed. The feeling in his gut was right. The kid who stood beside the *Peter Pan* poster slowly idled up the alley. Each time Relly stopped, the kid stopped. Each time Relly turned around, the kid looked behind him. He was attempting to be inconspicuous. Emphasis on "attempt."

"We've got company," Relly told the Squad.

Eight

Five and a half hours until Our Time

"**Have** you had the Café Edison's matzo ball soup? Everybody loves their matzo ball soup. I could live off their matzo ball soup!"

"Hudson, we don't even know if this café exists," Monica said as they navigated from the closed sewer. They walked farther away from Shubert Alley. The Café Edison was only two blocks over. From what Relly remembered in their present day, they should be at the café in less than five minutes.

The Café Edison sat along Forty-Seventh Street. It had a simple round awning with the café's name above the front door. Everybody from actors to choreographers, to bestselling authors stopped by to grab a bite to eat. Hudson recommended the Edison, being the foodie in the group.

"Oh, it exists, Monica. The Edison has been around for an eternity. Or at least a few decades."

What made the Edison even more special was that it was connected to the hotel next door. Relly once heard Thomas Edison himself had flicked on the hotel lights opening day. The café used to be the hotel's grandiose dining hall. Square pillars divided the room in half. Each one ornately decorated in spiraling motifs. The ceiling sprouted tiered chandeliers and a curved dome. Signed photographs from hundreds of Broadway stars graced the café's walls. Relly knew, one day in his future, his photo would be on that wall too. His autograph would be up for all of Broadway to read.

As the Squad walked closer, Relly couldn't help but wonder if there was no way home. Surely, there would have to be a way back, since there had been a way to get to the fifties. But what if there wasn't? And what would happen to his family? If Relly never stepped back through the front door at home, would he become a memory, just as his father was a memory? Would Bobby still go on to MIT? And Momma—Relly didn't want to think of how heartbroken Momma would be to not have her youngest around any longer.

"See! Told ya it exists," Hudson said as he opened the

door of the café. But as April and Hudson entered, Monica tapped Relly's shoulder.

"Hey, can I talk to you for a sec?"

"Sure!" Relly said, catching Hudson's eye as the door shut. "Grab us a table?" Relly asked. Hudson nodded.

Monica stepped left a few paces. Relly followed. When Monica stopped, so did Relly. Monica reached at her hair and began to twirl until a lock of brown strands was twisted around her finger. Then she shook her head, letting the strands unravel, loose.

"I had no idea, Relly," Monica said.

Relly shrugged. "About what?"

"About your grandfather. About how he wants you to take up engineering. How can a grandfather not want his grandson to follow his own dreams?" Monica reached for another lock of hair. Again, she began to twirl it around her finger.

"And it's making you doubt yourself." Monica shook her head. "I guess I'm saying this because my abuelita dropped everything for me to come to the city. And she didn't have to do that. Then, when I got the role, she decided to stay here with me. Families make sacrifices, and if I were in your shoes, I would feel so hurt." Monica paused, then she looked Relly in the eyes.

"Know what I tell my brother Freddy? Even though he's

all the way back in California, I tell him each night to look up at the stars and the moon. La luna y las estrellas. I love him as much as the universe. I tell him the universe is so big that we don't know how far it stretches. So are his dreams. Love your dreams like the universe, Relly."

Relly watched as a man in a gray suit exited the café. The man swiftly placed a matching hat on top of his head. He looked left, then right at the sidewalk curb before quickly crossing the street.

"Back at home, Freddy needs all the care and attention because of his episodes. Seizures. Our abuelita still decided to stick with me. She followed my dream like it was her own. That's sacrifice."

"I guess I do feel kind of hurt," said Relly. "You know how a kid feels when they drop their ice cream on the sidewalk? That's how I felt when Grandpa Gregory told me to find a backup plan. But Grandpa has seen a lot. He's been through a lot. From 1927 until now." Relly looked around. He took in the difference between his present New York City and 1958 New York City. There was a Woolworth store a few doors down, which did not exist in the future. A bright yellow taxi gently pulled up the street, but the car was different from those made in the future. A green-and-silver Coach bus rolled up to its stop. But it was a type of bus Relly had only seen in history books.

"In Grandpa's mind, he's only trying to help me."

Monica nodded and let the strand of hair loose. "Love your dreams like the universe, Relly."

"Love your dreams like the universe," Relly repeated.

"If you ever want to talk, you know my phone's always on," said Monica. "Except for now!" She glanced at Relly's backpack. Relly laughed.

Inside, Relly and Monica found April and Hudson seated at a wooden booth with brown cushions. Around them, glasses clinked, forks clashed. Talking and chatter erupted from the surrounding booths as the waiter took their orders. The café wasn't crowded on this day, but it wasn't empty, either. There was a nice in-between, which Relly hoped meant no one would overhear their conversation.

"Does anyone even know what happened in the fifties?" Hudson asked as he glanced over the paper menu. "1958 doesn't ring any bells for me."

"Oh!" April picked up a napkin and started to fold it into a neat square. Relly noticed April needed a way to occupy her hands without her phone. "I do! Listen, history is my favorite subject."

"You couldn't have told us that before we entered this decade?" Hudson said sarcastically.

"If I had known we would end up here, then yes. Anyway," April began, "NASA started in the fifties. Andy

Warhol got his art career going in the fifties. *Porgy and Bess* was recorded in the fifties. Barbie was invented. How do I know that? Ask my little sister. Oh! And *Man from Planet X*, the movie, one of my dad's favorites."

Relly knew April could keep going. Good thing she stopped talking when the waiter walked over. The waiter's eyes lingered a little longer on the clothes the Squad wore. Fashion of the 1950s wasn't too far off from what they usually wore. Still, their T-shirts and sweatshirts definitely didn't look like they were from the fifties. Relly had a feeling they gave off the look of something that did not belong.

The waiter narrowed his eyebrows and cleared his throat. He held up a pencil and notepad, still eyeing the Squad's clothes.

"Chef's special today is the matzo ball soup," said the waiter.

"Matzo ball soup!" shouted Hudson "See, I told you!"

Once they placed their orders, the waiter said it would be fifteen minutes until they received their food. But when Relly saw the waiter walking back with a full round tray, it had only been five.

"Tea and matzo ball soup," the waiter said when he returned. He placed April's and Monica's dishes in front of them. Steam billowed from their bowls.

"Pastrami on rye." He set down Hudson's sandwich. Hudson rubbed his hands together.

"Now that's what I call a sandwich!"

"And cheese blintzes for you," said the waiter. He set the pancake-type dish in front of Relly and quickly maneuvered the empty tray so it was now placed underneath his armpit.

"Anything else I can get you folks? Salt? Sugar? Pepper? Ice cream? Clothing without writing on the front? Kids these days," the waiter said under his breath. "I cannot keep up with the fashion."

"No, thanks! This all looks great," Relly blurted, already stuffing his fork with food. The waiter smiled and started up the aisle, taking an order at another table. Relief swept over Relly's face. Relly wanted to get back to the visions, clues, pieces to a mysterious puzzle.

Relly reached for his water. He held up the cool glass, about to take a sip. Then his eyes darted to the door. It chimed as it opened, then closed. When Relly glanced at the entrance, the same kid from the alley stood inside the front door. Relly slumped down in his seat. He dragged his backpack so it was now almost over his head.

"What are you doing?" Hudson hissed. Relly slumped lower. Hudson followed, slumping down into the cushion. Monica did the same from the opposite side of the booth.

"That kid's been following us," Relly whispered.

"What kid?" Hudson whispered back.

"The one from the alley. Are you even paying attention?"

"It's hard to concentrate when I'm hungry!"

"Hey! Party under the table!" April peeked her head below. "What's up? I want in." Relly sat back up and placed his backpack in the empty seat beside him.

"You think he's caught on?" Hudson asked, now back above the table.

"To what? Us being from the future? No. But I think it's time I found out what exactly he wants." Relly took a sip of his water. The kid at the door took his cap off. He rubbed his hands together to get them warm.

"Maybe he's lost," Monica suggested, dipping her fork into her food.

"Or it's just a coincidence. Those happen," said April. "Right? Why would he be following us?"

Relly shook his head.

"Don't know, but I do know he wants something. As a younger brother, I know the look of a kid who wants something. I invented that look." Relly scooted out of the booth. "Maybe he's been trying to get our attention and we've been too oblivious to notice." With that, Relly walked past their booth and the next. He walked to the front door. At the door, Relly scooted past a customer leaving. Finally, he reached the mystery kid.

"You hungry?" Relly asked. "Thirsty? Lost? If so, don't feel bad, because we're kind of lost too." Relly waited for the kid to answer.

"No," came the soft word out the boy's mouth. "None of that." If Relly hadn't been paying attention, he wouldn't have even heard.

"Well . . ." Relly hesitated. He didn't really know what to do or say. But he did know he could not have a random kid follow them around all day. "You want to sit with us? There's room at our table." Once again, Relly found himself waiting for the kid to respond. Finally, the boy nodded.

At the table, the child squeezed in between Hudson and Relly, across from Monica and April. Hudson sliced off half his sandwich and slid it to the kid. The kid took one bite of Hudson's sandwich, then one sip of a lone glass of water on the table. He held the half-eaten sandwich in his hands, on the verge of digging in again. Then the kid put the sandwich back on Hudson's plate. Hudson grimaced.

"Dad calls me Lloyd," the kid said. He looked up at Relly with the same large eyes. Relly's whole body felt warm. His dad's name was Lloyd too. "I got flyers," he said, beaming. "Bunches of flyers. Wanna see 'em? Wanna come to my dad's show? Oh, please say you do!" Lloyd pulled his satchel up onto his lap and opened the clasp. Inside, Relly could see hundreds of half slips of paper. Each bundled in neat stacks. Lloyd pulled out a flyer for Relly and the Squad to look at.

"Call me Harlem's newsboy. Deliverer of Harlem's most extraordinary events. Or some sort. I spread news about our tap shows. We call them Round the Worlds."

The newsboy reference immediately made Relly think of the Broadway musical *Newsies*. Hudson let out in a low whisper, "Now is the time to seize the day!"

"Round the Worlds?"

Lloyd nodded to the flyer.

SLYDE
AT HARLEM'S LAFAYETTE THEATER!
MARCH 6, 1958
8 P.M.

Relly gasped as he reached for the flyer. He held his breath, pulling the paper close. He immediately recognized the name. When he breathed out, Relly knew it was the same name the instructor had said to the kid in one of the visions. On the flyer was a black-and-white image of a man tap-dancing on stage. Relly recognized that man, too. He was the one from the bodega. He was Slyde.

Nine

Five hours until Our Time

"**Round** the World. A four-week tour when tap dancers perform at different venues. Round the Worlds start in Harlem, they go off to Philadelphia to perform at the Standard. Then they head to Baltimore. Ever been to Baltimore?"

Relly nodded. He had, for a family vacation. Grandpa Gregory had come along too.

"Well, the theater there is called the Royal. Then the dancers head to one last stop in Washington, DC. But you know what really gets me frosted?"

"Frosted?" Hudson asked.

"Daddy can perform at some of these venues, but some places won't even let Black folks sit in the audience. If

Daddy wants to get a bite to eat after the show, they make him go backstage or off premises. Ain't that a trip?" Lloyd stuffed the flyer back in his satchel. He sat up straight and puffed out his chest. "That's why he likes to perform at these theaters during Round the Worlds. They are all Black venues, so he doesn't have to worry about folks telling him off for being in the wrong dressing room. Some folks think segregation is only in the South; it is not."

"What other dancers are there, Lloyd?" Relly asked.

"There's Bunny Briggs, you'll know him when you see his eyes. Has tap style that's real delicate. Got legs that move like an earthquake. Then there's Peg Leg Bates; Clayton's his real name. You've probably seen him on the *Ed Sullivan Show*. The sound his taps make is different all 'cause of his special leg. He's acrobatic with his steps. Then there's my dad, Slyde." Lloyd waved. "Guess what he's known for!"

"Slides!" said Relly.

"How'd you know?" asked Lloyd.

"I think I've seen him before."

"Well, that's just copacetic. Say, you wanna come to the Lafayette? You wanna see my dad perform? You wanna see Slyde slide? You wanna go to the best theater in New York City? I like to think of it as Harlem's littlest big secret."

"Yes!" Relly said, louder than what he intended.

"Well, it's my job to find people to attend the show. I

gotta warn you, though. My dad, Slyde, he's got the pits."

"The pits?" Hudson asked.

"Down in the dumps, understand? Feels he's losing his flow, get me?"

"Why?" Relly asked, scraping up the last bit of food on his plate.

"All 'cause he thinks people don't want to see or hear tap anymore. He's starting to think he should try out a new career. Folks are now listening to that electric, rocking noise with that guy—what's his name?"

"Elvis!" Hudson hollered.

"Elvis?" Lloyd repeated. "No, I'm talking about Jackie Brenston and his Delta Cats. Got a song called 'Rocket 88.' They play at the venue across from the Lafayette. And Daddy's all but quit over it."

Relly did not want to wait any longer. He shoved the last of his food down and pulled out the change Bobby had given him Tuesday night to pay. Five dollars and a quarter.

"Ooh! Shiny quarter!" said Lloyd. "I have a flower collection and a yo-yo collection. Think I should start a quarter collection?" Lloyd began to reach for the change. Relly quickly swiped the five-dollar bill and quarter off the table.

"No!" said Relly, gripping the change in his hand tight.

"Jeez, you four are a serious bunch."

"What Relly means is . . ." Monica winked at Relly. "You

don't want change pulled from somebody's pocket. What fun is there in that? What you want is sidewalk change. Makes for a better story when you tell people how you started your collection, Lloyd."

"Yeah!" said Relly. "Monica is right. Bet you will find a ton on our way to see Slyde. Imagine, Lloyd . . . shiny pennies, shiny nickels, shiny dimes!"

Lloyd jumped in his seat, scrambling to get out of the booth. "What are we waiting for?" Lloyd asked, already walking up the aisle. Monica, Hudson, and April laughed as they followed Lloyd. Relly tossed the change back on the table and ran after them. He did not want to give the waiter any chance to ask why their money was from the future.

Then Relly and the Squad followed Lloyd to the front door. Relly took one last look at the photos and autographs on the walls of the Café Edison. At least now he knew he wasn't the only one to have doubts.

At the nearest subway station, the Squad and Lloyd waited for the next train. Relly thought it was risky to leave Manhattan without finding a way to get home. But now that he knew where to find the man he saw in his visions, Relly was not going to pass up the opportunity.

"His show starts at eight," Hudson whispered to Relly as they ran down the subway steps. "Our show starts at eight!"

"We'll be quick. We won't even wait to see the show. Just let me talk to him, please."

Relly needed to see Slyde. The real Slyde, not the version he saw when he touched the sliver of wood. There had to be a bigger reason behind why he could see these visions of this man dancing. Relly needed to find that out too.

When the subway train arrived, it beat against the steel tracks. The subway came to a screeching halt. The silver steel door slid open. As the Squad took their seats, the subway pulled off. First it slowly inched away from the platform before it picked up more speed. The train ticked along the tracks.

There was something peculiar about being in a retro subway car going to Harlem. Going home. The train was an everyday occurrence, but this time it felt off. Bobby wasn't with Relly. And when they got off the subway, would Relly even recognize Harlem? One with no Bobby, or Juanita's, Grandpa Gregory, or Momma? Relly swallowed the tingle that had grown in his throat. He closed his eyes, taking in a deep breath. He hoped he was making the right decision. Was it a selfish decision to go to Harlem? When Relly released his breath, his mind turned back to the Squad and Lloyd.

"Why were you following us?"

"Huh?" Lloyd asked. April, Monica, and Hudson looked from Relly to Lloyd, Lloyd to Relly. "You were following us. It was obvious. Why?"

"It wasn't in a strange way. I'm no weirdo."

"I think we deserve to know."

Lloyd paused as if he was trying to precisely gather the right words to say. "I followed you because you look like friends."

"Friends?" Monica asked. Lloyd nodded. Relly saw a few tears come to April's eyes.

"I want to be one, a friend," said Lloyd. "And you looked the way friends are supposed to look. At least, you do to me." With that, Lloyd's eyes got big. It reminded Relly of how he looks at his older brother, especially when he wants something.

"I don't have any." Lloyd paused. "Friends."

The train picked up speed and started to careen around a bend. Relly knew they were getting closer to Harlem as the Squad and Lloyd grabbed on to a silver pole to keep their balance.

"This flyer thing keeps me busy." Lloyd patted his satchel. "Then, when I'm not working, I'm in the garden."

"Garden?" Relly leaned forward. As the train slowed into the 125th Street station, Relly thought about how his dad used to bring him up to their garden. The one on the rooftop. The one that didn't exist anymore. When they got back, if they got back, maybe Relly could restore it.

As they came out of the subway, a breeze hit Relly. It was the sharp, vivid sensation of déjà vu. It was the feeling of being someplace before, this place before. In the future. Relly could sense the subway take off underneath their feet. The train below thudded between the concrete tunnels. Then he turned his attention forward. The movement of people walking up and down Lenox Avenue was a non-stop conveyor belt. A stroll leisurely and determined. The sight of Harlem filled Relly's mind and soul with a thrill.

"Shouldn't that say Malcolm X Boulevard?" Hudson pointed to the sign that said LENOX AVENUE. Relly already knew even in the future, the street went by both names.

Storefront shops lined Lenox. There was Frank's Fish Market with fresh fish placed on blocks of ice. Underneath the ice were wooden boxes. This was all behind a pristine clean glass window. There was an optician's next door with a sign that announced their newest sale:

BUY 2 SPECTACLES FOR THE COST OF 1!
ONLY $10

"What a deal," said Monica. "Abuelita would say that's a price you can't beat."

Two doors down were stores for meats and poultry, next to a store that sold twenty-five-cent lunches with all the fixings. Chef Hudson was in his element.

"I'm in heaven," he said, swooning over a perfect cut of meat.

"No, Hudson. You're in Harlem," said Relly. The cafeteria was next to a candy store, and the candy store was next to a soda store. The soda store was next to a barber, and the barber was next to a Davin's Tailors.

"That's Richard's, my barber," said Lloyd, nodding back to the barbershop. Through the glass windows, Relly could see a barber wrapping a man's head with a warm towel.

"Richard's?" asked Relly, looking back at the red-and-white sign painted across the glass window. It was the same one Relly was used to walk past when he and Bobby met Momma at the diner.

"He cuts it low, like this. See?" Lloyd took off his hat and rubbed his head with his palm. Forward, then backward, as if his palm were an invisible brush. Backward, then forward. Lloyd plopped his cap back on his head.

Relly glanced at the Squad. Monica had stopped to wave and coo at a giggling baby in a black-and-silver stroller. April was already three storefronts ahead, admiring the flat-as-pancakes hats shaped like seashells. Cadillac Coupes de Ville and Chevrolet Bel Airs glided up and down the avenue. Cars with sloping rooftops and bumpers shaped like fins. Hudson stopped and stared with his mouth wide. He gawked at the vehicles as if they were treats baked for his *Broadway Sizzlers* FoodTube show.

"Richard's Barbershop is where my dad used to take me,"

Relly began. "It's one of the only memories I have of him. To be honest, I think it's the last memory I have of him."

Lloyd's face drooped. Relly felt awkward. But now that Relly had started, he couldn't stop.

"The first time my dad took me to get my hair cut, I was three. When the barber was ready, Dad sat me on his lap. I remember that feeling of being safe like it was yesterday." The only other person he'd told was Bobby. Bobby had more memories of their dad, but when Bobby tried to tell Relly about their father, his stories never felt real. Not like Relly's own.

"So where are we going and how do we get there?" Relly changed the subject.

"To the Lafayette," said Lloyd. "You know, it's sometimes called 'the House Beautiful.'"

"And this is where Slyde is?" asked Relly.

"First stop on his Round the World tour."

"All right, kiddo," said April, now back beside Relly and Lloyd. "We have the deets, you lead the way," April said, taking a cue from Jimmy the doorman.

"Peachy! We take a left on 132nd. You can't miss the Lafayette at the corner."

It was ironic to Relly how they went back over sixty years, yet some places, like Richard's Barbershop, hadn't even changed.

Ten

Four hours until Our Time

132nd Street and Seventh Avenue was a packed corner of Harlem. People waited on the sidewalks and people waited in half of the street. People stood under an awning of bright round lights and people streamed in and out of two solid theater doors. Clear glass windows showed straight through to a crowded lobby. Inside, Relly could see more folks standing shoulder to shoulder. Those same folks hugged the curb outside the theater, carefully dodging cars that streamed up and down the street. The air was thick with laughter and excitement.

Those same people were dressed in their best, like the people in decked-out fancy clothes Relly saw in his first vision at the bodega. As Relly and the Squad walked closer, Relly saw the building's name lit up, bright letters fashioned in big balls of light.

LAFAYETTE

This theater reminded Relly of the Apollo a few blocks over. The Apollo, he knew, was prized and special. On a marquee were names of each performer for the day's show.

Bunny Briggs
Peg Leg Bates
The Nicholas Brothers
Slyde

"We can go around the side to the stage door. Don't call it a back door, Dad doesn't like that. But it's much faster that way. Would take us forever to get through all these people if we walked through the front," Lloyd said.

As Lloyd, Hudson, April, and Monica walked the edge of the theater, Relly couldn't believe he was about to see the man from his visions. A literal dream come true. Relly took a moment to savor the scene. With time short, they still did not have a way home. Once they got inside the Lafayette, the Squad would have to be quick.

"Relly!" Hudson yelled.

"I'm coming!"

As Relly ran to catch up with his friends, he had a sense

of déjà vu again. Past the front of the Lafayette Theater and around to the side of the building, the feeling intensified.

"I've been here before," Relly told the Squad. The feeling hit Relly the closer he walked to the stage door.

"What!" the three other Squad members belted. A few people from the crowd turned to see where that "what" had come from.

"Wait, of course you have, Relly," said Monica. "It's Harlem. We've all been here before."

"No, that's not what I meant. I mean I know I've been in this exact spot." Relly racked his brain. Then the scent of cherries filled his nose. His mind went back to the shattered jar on the bodega floor.

"Nita's!" Juanita's Market stood in the exact same spot as the Lafayette Theater, almost seventy years in the future. The entrance to the stage door was the same as the entrance to Nita's.

Hudson let out a long, exaggerated, "Oooohhhh."

"What happened to it?"

"Dunno." Relly shrugged. "Guess lots of buildings get torn down when people don't need them anymore. Shame."

"Hey! You kids coming?"

"Who you calling kids?" April replied.

"We've got plenty of time before Dad goes on. You read the sign. Bunny Briggs. Peg Leg Bates. Those two brothers.

That's three whole acts before Slyde still—time's ticking!"

"Understatement much?" asked Hudson.

"Listen, buddy, Dad will wonder where I am. So if you want the good seats, best you follow me." Lloyd waved them to the stage door propped open with its own door-man. As Lloyd and the Squad entered, the doorman stood up from his seat. Relly thought the doorman was on the verge of asking who they were, and why they were entering backstage. Instead, he only tipped his hat, nodded, then let the Squad in.

"See you found some friends," the doorman said to Lloyd.

"Sure as day, Bert!"

Even inside, the density of people reminded Relly of the Squad's own opening night. Or any show, for that matter. There was even a stage manager who tapped a button to a nearby intercom.

"Fayard Nicholas, if you're in the building, please let me know. You're on in ten!"

Stagehands ran back and forth. There was a rush and exhilaration in the air. Passing dressing rooms and shoe rooms and makeup rooms, even the bathrooms, the thrill of being back inside a theater came to Relly. All this for the people in the seats. All this for each dancer and actor, every singer's dreams too. Lloyd turned to a closed door.

"Here we go." He inhaled as he knocked four times. Each interval between knocks was a code for the person on the other side. There was silence as they waited. Seconds turned to a full minute. A full minute turned to five.

"Is anyone in there?" Monica asked.

"He's coming," Lloyd replied. "Slyde, also known as my dad, is a man who likes to take his time." As they waited, Relly hadn't noticed the name on the dressing-room door. But as Hudson scooted to the side, now Relly had a full view of the name in gold cursive.

> *Gregory Morton*
> *Slyde*

"Huh? That's funny," Relly said under his breath. "My grandpa has that same name."

My grandpa has that same name.

Relly froze. This time it wasn't a vision that caused him to freeze in place. *Grandpa Gregory?* Relly thought as adrenaline began to rush through his veins.

"Grandpa Gregory Morton?" Relly said out loud.

"Your grandpa?" Hudson asked. April and Monica turned to look. Each read the name to themselves.

"I think so," Relly said. "I hope so. Wow, Grandpa Gregory is Slyde?" Relly crossed his fingers. Gregory Morton was the only Grandpa Relly knew. To come face-to-face with his grandfather in the past, Relly wondered if something in his own time would change. Maybe they shouldn't see who was on the opposite side of the dressing-room door. Hadn't Relly mentioned earlier not messing with the timeline? Surely seeing a younger version of his grandfather would compromise his future. Would Relly even exist whenever they found a way back?

Gregory "Slyde" Morton's door clicked unlocked. The knob began to turn. "Wait!" Relly blurted out loud. The wheels in Relly's mind kept churning. If Slyde was also Grandpa Gregory and Grandpa Gregory was also Gregory Morton, that meant Lloyd was related to Relly too.

"Dad?"

As the door cracked open, Lloyd pushed the dressing-room door forward. Then he let the Squad step inside. Gregory "Slyde" Morton stood beside the door as he lifted one leg up on a chair. He bent over with a rag in one hand, swiping left, swiping right, shining his black tap shoes. With each swipe came a dull, low squeak. As the Squad entered and Lloyd shut the door, Gregory "Slyde" Morton began on his other tap shoe.

"Lloyd Morton, I have been looking all over for you. The bathrooms, the balcony—I almost took the stage crew to look on the roof! The rooftop, Lloyd! Where in the world have you been?" The slightest bead of sweat dropped off

Slyde's nose. When it hit his left tap shoe, Slyde immediately swiped it off.

"Passing out your flyers, Dad. There's a crowd the size of Central Park out there, you know. You have me to thank for that." Lloyd puffed out his chest. The kid beamed.

"Ah. Always looking out for your pop. There's not a thing you don't think up."

"Guess where we went, Dad!" Lloyd did not wait for Gregory "Slyde" Morton to ask. "We started in Shubert Alley. Then we went to see Ethel Merman at her show. Then we went to the Café Edison for lunch. Yummo! Then you know what we did? We took a train to Harlem. I've showed them all of New York City! Isn't that neat? Isn't that grand? Isn't that peachy?"

"You left out that you followed us," said April.

"Me, Lloyd, the tour guide. Me, Lloyd, the paperboy. Lloyd, the garden expert extraordinaire."

Slyde shook his head as he gave Lloyd a pat on his back.

"You, Lloyd, the jack-of-all-trades." Slyde turned to the four kids crowded at the dressing-room door. His eyes went from Lloyd to the kids, then back to Lloyd again. "You forgot something. When were you going to introduce me?"

"Oh yeah! These are my friends. Nifty, huh? This is Hudson, Monica, April, and Relly. Don't they look cool?" Lloyd beamed at his new friends. Hudson rubbed his hand through his hair. He stood a little straighter at being called cool.

Slyde folded his rag into a neat square. Using his free hand, he began to shake the hands of the young Broadway stars. First he started with Hudson. Then on to April, followed by Monica. With each handshake, Slyde said, "Pleasure to meet you." On down the line, Relly felt each nerve in his body. Each nerve connected to his soul. The closer Slyde approached, Relly's palms were slick with sweat. Relly thought about running for the door before he shook Slyde's hand.

This younger version of his grandfather was slim, tall, and nimble. He had a voice that sounded almost the same, but not quite exact. This Slyde's voice didn't crack over his words. It was not riddled with doubtful questions, either.

"Remind me your name, son." Gregory "Slyde" Morton held out his hand.

"Relly."

"Relly. That's different. Fits you. Pleasure is all mine." Their two palms lifted and joined in a shake.

To be this far away from home yet in his own neighborhood, Relly felt overwhelmed. He wanted a hug. One like the hug he had given his grandfather back home after the Tuesday evening show. One like the hug his grandfather always gave to Relly, even if he did have a complaint on his tongue. Relly took a step closer. He opened his arms and wrapped them around Gregory "Slyde" Morton. Relly squeezed tight.

"All right! Very good. All right, now." Gregory laughed. "Man, did I need that today."

"Why's that, Dad?" Lloyd asked as the Squad took a seat.

"Because the gig is up." Gregory tossed the rag into a nearby trash can. In the time the Squad had been in the room, Lloyd had already set his satchel down and laid out flyers. He thumbed through each one, counting them as Slyde let out an exhausted sigh.

"I am tired, kiddo."

"Let it all out, Dad," Lloyd said in reply. "That's what you tell me to do."

"I'm starting to think my momma was right. I should have stuck with playing the violin. You kids seem like a smart bunch. Let me clue you in. You got that venue across the street, playing rock and roll. You got some places that don't even want me to eat with my fans on account of the color of my skin. You got competition left and right. Know the effect all that has on a performer? It wears you down. I don't know if this industry is for me. Truth be told, I don't even think I want to find out." Slyde went over to a table and picked up a brush. He began to brush his hair the same way Lloyd had brushed his earlier.

The smile Gregory "Slyde" Morton had greeted the Squad with was replaced with a flat, blank line. Slyde's demeanor dropped and deflated. It even seemed the lights in the dressing room dimmed.

"I think I know why I'm here," Relly whispered to April, Monica, and Hudson. Slyde sat next to his son, counting flyers. "And that means I know why I saw those visions, too."

The Squad waited for Relly to continue. He pulled off his backpack and pulled out the notebook. Relly opened it and started to write.

"In the future, our future, Grandpa was trying to get me to find a backup plan. Clearly, Grandpa Gregory, *Slyde*, has his own worries, and I need to get him to not give up. I need to get him to not lose sight of his dream. If Grandpa gives up now, he'll be miserable the rest of his life. He'll take that misery out on me and my dreams."

"But how are you going to do that?" Hudson asked. "Remember, if you change anything, we're kaput. Obsolete. We'll probably be stuck in the fifties forever."

"We've already changed so much, though," Relly said. "First of all, we came here. Then we met Ethel Merman. Then we ate actual nineteen-fifties food at a café, which was tasty. Then I get to talk to my dad. My dad! If anything were to change in our future, we've already made it happen."

Slyde stood and grabbed the flyers off the table. He

stuffed them back in Lloyd's satchel, messing up Lloyd's count. The kid looked like he was about to burst out in tears until he blinked, wiped a tear from his face, got up, and followed his father. They walked to the dressing-room door.

"We're going home. You kids feel free to see the other acts today. Heard those Nicholas Brothers sure are a sight. All jumping and jiving and that."

"Home? You're leaving? You have a full house. It's packed! We saw the people. They are here for you!" Relly said.

"A packed house means you're doing something right," said Monica.

"Didn't you see the other names? There are three whole acts before me. That's who those people came to see."

"But you can't give up. What if you regret it in the future?" Relly asked.

Slyde shook his head as Lloyd opened the dressing-room door. "I'll deal with it then is what," Slyde said as he stepped out. Father and son walked out of the dressing room and up the narrow hall together. As they approached the Lafayette's stage door, the Squad ran behind them, trying to catch up.

"You're making a mistake!" Relly yelled. In the future, his grandfather wouldn't just "deal with it." But by the time the Squad reached the door, Gregory "Slyde" Morton and Lloyd were out of eyesight.

Eleven

5:00 P.M.
Three hours until Our Time

"*That* was not what I expected and too bad my phone's not working. Imagine this as a post on Insta. Hashtag 'what just happened?!' Hashtag 'Slyde who?' Hashtag 'why did he just leave?'" April said as they edged around the Lafayette. Relly could no longer see Lloyd and Slyde. Even though the crowd had thinned, and most people were now inside, there was still a swarm of people waiting on the sidewalk. Slyde and Lloyd could have been in the midst of that crowd, or they could have walked up any part of Seventh Avenue.

"How could we get this close? I feel like someone's yanked a rug from under me," Relly said as they passed a tree. Its twisted branches reminded Relly of cinnamon sticks. The way each leaf spread along the branches resembled fingertips across piano keys. Or dark green flags waving in the wind. Each leaf rustled as the Squad walked past.

"Did you think he would kick us out?"

"Slyde did not kick us out, April," said Hudson.

"Well, that's what it feels like. Right, guys? I'm kinda embarrassed. I've never had a performer quit in front of me before. We've come all this way to see him, right, Relly? I was looking forward to seeing him perform. You know what I heard someone say when we first walked up to this theater?" April didn't wait for the Squad to respond. "They said, 'Neato!' Isn't that a fun old-school word? Anyway, it's *neato* Relly gets to see visions of people dancing. What do we get to see? Nothing. Zero. Zip. Not a thing. I wanted to see what Relly saw."

"Neato?" asked Monica.

"I'm going to add it to my vocab."

A slight murmur of music escaped from the theater. The music was for the other set of performers. The ones who went on before Slyde. The music crept through the front door and floated out onto the street. But there was no use in standing, waiting. For what? Slyde and Lloyd had already left for home. And Relly didn't think home meant the apartment building on 119th Street. Had it even been built yet?

"I think we need to get to our time—no pun intended. What else is there for us to see here?" said Hudson. "We only have three hours left." All four looked toward a nearby outdoor clock attached to the wall of a building across the street. The hands were at five after five. Relly imagined Claudia Middleton carefully opening her notebook. Carefully waiting to scribble down the exact moment Relly failed to walk through the stage door. Then he imagined his grandfather at home, on the couch. Grandpa Gregory struggled to move, and he would be using every ounce of energy to get ready to watch the Thursday evening *Our Time* performance. The next thought that popped into Relly's mind was young Grandpa Gregory, at his home in this Harlem. Giving up.

"No," said Relly. "Not yet. We can't leave right now. I've seen too many of those visions so far to leave now."

"Yeah, the three clues?" asked Monica. Relly could sense the panic pulsing through Hudson at that moment. He saw the panic at being stuck in 1958 all over Hudson's face the longer they stayed in the fifties. But still, leaving was not the option.

"April, you were in *Aladdin*. How many wishes did the genie give?" Relly asked.

"Three. Duh. That's preschool, Relly. Everyone knows that. Three wishes in *Aladdin*. Three acts in a play. Three primary colors. Three Stooges. Three sides to a triangle."

"We get it!" shouted Hudson.

"She was making a point," said Monica.

"*My* point is," said Relly, "that most clues or wishes come in threes, right? So right now I have three pieces to some puzzle. I mean, come on. I saw my grandfather up on a stage dancing his heart out. Then I saw him learning how to dance from someone who was clearly an expert. Then I saw his mom telling him to quit on his own dream. And there has to be a reason for all of them. I'm missing that reason."

The Squad took in Relly's words. As they stood beside the tree, Relly dug in his backpack and pulled out his tap shoes. Relly kept the tap shoes inside his backpack just in case he needed to practice between shows. He held them up while he placed his palm against the tree for balance.

"You know what these mean to me? I put them on and they turn to wings. They take me across a stage, but in my head, these shoes take me anyplace I want to go. On top of Harlem, on top of my craziest dreams. But you know where else they take me? Back with my dad. When I put these on, I am always closer to him. Grandpa Gregory feels that way in his tap shoes too. In that vision with his mom, he said so. He said that when he taps, he flies. Just like me." Relly removed his hand from the tree. He put his tap shoes back inside his backpack. "That's why I can't let him give up."

"All right, all right!" said Hudson. "But six on the dot, we're out. We can't stay here any longer. The farther away we are from Shubert Alley and the hole we came out of, the harder it will be to get back. Plus, Selena Gomez, Relly! Selena Gomez will be on my cooking show! If I miss *Our Time*, what will Selena Gomez think?!"

"You said her name a dozen times," said April.

"And I'll say it a dozen more! Selena . . ." Hudson inhaled. "Gomez!" Hudson exhaled.

Relly nodded. Hudson was right. They would stay until six, which gave them less than one hour. Any longer and they would have to leave, no matter if Relly had found the answers for those visions or not.

"Who is that?" Monica asked. The Squad swiveled and aimed their sight in the direction of a shiny black Cadillac. It pulled to the curb and stopped in front of the theater. The car lights shut off and the driver door opened. Decked out in a three-piece suit and tie, the driver walked to the back door. He held out his hand for the person inside to take. Relly immediately recognized the driver as young Jimmy Onions.

"Jimmy!" the Squad shouted in unison.

"Well, young Jimmy," said Hudson. "He can drive? Wow, things really were different in the fifties." But the young Ethel Merman doorman in training did not respond. Instead, the person inside the car grabbed his hand. Ethel Merman slid from the back seat and stepped out of the old-school car. Her red sequined dress sparkled against the lights from the Lafayette. The people who still stood in line swiveled their heads to look.

"What's Ethel doing here?" Monica asked.

"What are they both doing here?" Relly wanted to know. A song of Ethel's popped into Relly's head. It was one from the Broadway musical *Gypsy*.

You'll be swell! You'll be great!

"Unless everything's coming up roses," Relly said as Jimmy and Ethel walked up to the theater entrance. Ethel glided past the Squad. But when she caught a quick glimpse of the four kids, Ethel stopped and turned around.

"You!" she said. That one word felt like thunder against Relly's ears. "Sonny, aren't they the kids who were at my stage door earlier?"

Young Jimmy nodded to Ethel.

"Thought as much. I never forget a face. Or four." Ethel's words were broad paint strokes scribbling sentences into the Harlem air.

"Quite a ruckus you all caused in Midtown." Her string of pearls shimmered under the lights. "But I was pulled away before I could get a word out. Still don't know if I believe your story. The future, huh?" Ethel walked toward the tree. She lifted a hand to touch it.

As her hand and the tree met, Ethel rubbed gentle circles. "I've always wanted to be in a musical about the future. Say, I'll give you kids a few words of advice. I'll tell you what my mother used to tell me. Wherever home happens to be, my wish is for you to make it there."

With that, Ethel clicked her fingers. Young Jimmy looped his arm around Ethel's, still paying no mind to the four kids. Ethel and Jimmy walked up to the entrance of the Lafayette, then disappeared through the front door.

Relly had to find a place to go. A location where they would not be pointed out by a crowd. Somewhere mellow. Somewhere quiet. A spot where they would not be identified as looking out of place. As they walked away from the corner and up 132nd Street, Relly turned them toward the direction of Lenox Avenue.

The street was lined with churches and hair salons. Clothing stores and apartments above restaurants. Relly had in mind a building he knew was only three blocks away. The structure sat on a corner, just as the Lafayette Theater sat on a corner.

After his father passed away, Relly had felt an emptiness travel through his body. No matter how much he tried to fill that emptiness with hugs from Momma or jokes from

Bobby, that hole poked. Some days, it felt like it was poking Relly's soul. Sure, he was only three, almost four when he lost his dad; still, Relly knew loss. He felt loss. He held it in his hand and rolled it in a ball and tried to throw the loss away. But the emptiness always came back.

Relly and Bobby spent their weekends at the library after their father passed. There, Relly pulled books off the shelf. Some days, Relly didn't even read the words on the pages. He looked at the pictures, using his imagination to pretend Dad was beside him, reading too. Relly let the books fill those holes back up. Finally, Momma's hugs started to help again. Bobby's jokes started to mend. Then, the library and its books had their own way of fixing Relly's broken heart too.

"One hour in the Schomburg," said Relly, continuing to walk up Lenox Avenue. "Then, if we can't find any answers, we go back to Midtown and we get home." The Squad agreed. They still had some time left. It wasn't quite six o'clock.

"Schomburg Division of Negro Literature, History and Prints," Relly whispered as he read the building's sign. The Squad approached a single three-story off-white building. 103 West 135th Street. The setting evening sun bounced off the building's glass windows. Relly caught his reflection. Yep, his hair was still pink and purple. Not even anyone in 1958 had a complaint about his vibrant hair. The time had changed, the decade had changed, but at least something about him was still the same.

Lush, thick green vines seemed to be superglued to the building facade. They began along the sides, then wrapped round the building edge. With each story, the vines became thick and bulky. Relly did not recall the Schomburg looking that way in the future. The green vines made the outside of the library look as if there was a botanical garden stuck in the middle of Harlem.

"Boston ivy," Relly said as he opened the library's front door. He thought about the vines that used to grow along his apartment rooftop. Relly and the Squad stepped inside.

Named after the Afro–Puerto Rican collector-curator-historian Arturo Alfonso Schomburg, the building was an encyclopedia. Words, phrases, paragraphs, pictures, music. Black life in America and across the world, all brought to this building in Harlem by Arturo Alfonso himself.

"I took a field trip here once," said April, eyes wide as their shoes echoed off the tile floors. The building felt sacred. "Well, not here here, but future here. I remember my teacher saying Alfonso wanted the world to know that Black people have a rich history, so he collected all types of items, then he made sure his collection stayed in Harlem."

"Children, may I offer my assistance?" A librarian with

shoulder-length curls and a black dress approached. Her smile slid smooth across her face. In her hands were a pen and slim slip of paper. JEAN BLACKWELL HUTSON was the name on the badge pinned to her dress. Before Relly could get his question out, the others were ready to ask theirs.

"Where are your portraits?"

"I heard there's a theater in the basement. Is that true? Can you show us? Why doesn't every library have a theater in its basement?"

"Can I sit where James Baldwin sat when he used to come here to read? My abuelita told me that."

Ms. Hutson wrote down each answer to Hudson's, April's, and Monica's questions. As Hudson, April, and Monica grabbed their slips of paper from Ms. Hutson, they all went off in separate directions. Relly had not thought his friends may have wanted to look up information at this library too.

"Everyone has a question. It's my job to make sure we have the answer. How can I be of assistance to you today?" Ms. Hutson turned to Relly.

Relly stumbled over the right words. He knew what and who he was looking for, but how to word it for a librarian to help? In the future, it would be simple to walk over to a computer and open its catalog. Search the internet for an answer. Bam! Hundreds, maybe thousands of solutions, right in front of him. There was no internet in the fifties. And how would a librarian know where to point Relly in the direction of answers to some random visions?

"I'm looking for information on a man," Relly began. He took a deep inhale. He wanted to pull out the three pieces of wood and see if Ms. Hutson had an answer for those, too.

"What's this man's name? We have biographies and autobiographies. We have nonfiction and newspapers. Give me a name; I'm positive it's in here somewhere. I'll see what I can find."

"Slyde," Relly blurted out.

"Slyde?"

"You know him?"

Ms. Hutson scribbled words on her notepad. "Gregory 'Slyde' Morton? Everybody knows Slyde. He's a marvel around here, isn't he?"

Relly nodded. If only Slyde believed those words too. Ms. Hutson tore the paper off and handed it to Relly. Relly looked down at the cursive writing in his hand.

"There you'll find the information you are looking for. If you don't, give me a holler." Ms. Hutson cupped Relly's fingers. She gave his closed hands and the paper inside a gentle pat. When Ms. Hutson walked away, Relly opened his palms. He read the call number, the coordinate to find the information he was looking for. Following the directions

Ms. Hutson had written down, Relly went up the steps to the second floor.

Upstairs, round wooden tables sprawled across the room. Large floor-to-ceiling windows lit up the space with natural light. Out the window, Relly could even see some of those green vines that covered the exterior facade.

"The children's room?" Relly muttered after he stepped inside. Several kids looked up from their spots at tables. One lifted a finger to her mouth and let out a stern "Shhh." Another librarian was seated behind a rectangular desk at the front of the room. She nodded to Relly as he entered.

Ms. Hutson had written, *Children's room, second floor. Theater, music, and dance section. Second shelf,* plus an extremely long call number with dots and letters and zeros.

"History. Folktales. Mathematics. Mythology," Relly whispered as he glanced at the shelves attached to walls. On top of each one was the name of the section in bold. Then his eyes saw another label. The one written on Ms. Hutson's paper.

"Theater, Music, Dance." Relly eyed the rows of books. Eight whole shelves, top to bottom with books. The very top shelf was stacked full of newspapers. Relly looked at the call number once again. He slid his finger across the length of the number, then looked to the shelf to find a match. The last book on the shelf was for Relly.

The room settled into a deeper silence. Relly sat at an empty table. He placed the book entitled *The Sound of Harlem* on top of the table. Then he slowly opened to the first page. It was a page full of so many words, but it wasn't the letters combined to make sentences that caught Relly's attention. What caught his attention were two black-and-white images. One of a tree. The other of a street. Underneath both pictures were the words:

Boulevard of Dreams
Tree of Hope

Relly gasped. He pulled his backpack up on the table, reached inside, and took out the three pieces of wood. Relly thought back to less than an hour ago, when the Squad had stood outside the Lafayette Theater. Could the pieces be from that same tree?

Relly wanted to shout. He wanted to jump on top of the table and hold up the book. He wanted to scream, "LOOK WHAT I FOUND!" But the kids were some serious studiers. Relly closed the book. He sat at the table and stared across the room. *Why is everyone so quiet?* Relly wondered if they could feel the same excitement that was building up inside of him. He had to tell the Squad, stat. Relly placed the book back on the shelf. When he turned around, April, Monica, and Hudson had entered the room. Clearly, they had been looking for him.

"Did you know there's a theater in this library? Did you know Harry Belafonte and Sidney Poitier come here? Here! The legends! I feel as if I'm in history."

"You are in history, April," said Hudson.

"Shhh!" whispered a nearby child studying a book on mathematics.

"I think I know what to do with these pieces of wood," Relly told them. He caught himself smiling as he stuffed the pieces in his backpack.

"What? How?" Hudson asked. Relly ushered the Squad into the hallway. There, they could talk without whispered shushes and glancing eyes.

"Did you see another vision?" asked Monica. "What was it, Relly?"

Relly shook his head. "There was this book called *The Sound of Harlem*. When I opened it, I saw that tree."

"What tree?" Hudson asked.

"Harlem's tree, smack in the middle of Harlem's Boulevard of Dreams . . . Harlem's wishing Tree of Hope."

It still seemed as if Hudson, April, and Monica were lost. Relly continued, "You know what this means?" April, Monica, and Hudson shook their heads. "It means wood plus tree and tree plus boulevard equals answers."

"Answers to what, Relly? Answers to what? To why our phones don't work? Or why we were sent here in the first place? Or why the fifties are actually starting to grow on me?"

"No, April," Relly said as the Squad walked down the library steps. They waved goodbye to Ms. Hutson as they stepped outside of the Schomburg's doors. "I'll explain when we get back to the Tree of Hope."

Twelve

7:00 P.M.

One hour until Our Time

Why *didn't I realize this sooner?*

Relly had passed the Tree of Hope before. Each time Relly and Bobby walked to the bodega, or walked to the library, or walked to the restaurant Momma worked at, if they took 131st Street, the Tree of Hope stood in the middle of the intersection. Only, Relly never recognized it as a wooden tree. In the future the Tree of Hope was not made of wood and bark. It did not stand at thirty feet tall. In the future, the tree was a blue, orange, yellow, and green statue. The real tree had been replaced when its wood started to die. Part of that tree stood on the stage at the Apollo. Relly even remembered seeing performers rub the stump for good luck before going on.

Harlem's Boulevard of Dreams was also known as Seventh Avenue. It was the same street that was home to the Lafayette, the same street where the Tree of Hope stood in the fifties. This time, when Relly and the Squad walked back toward the theater, Relly understood why the street was called Boulevard of Dreams. Anyone who came up Seventh Avenue had a dream, a vision, a hope.

For so many dancers and singers, musicians and artists, the Lafayette was where they got their start. It was Harlem and the theater that accepted them for who they were, regardless of the color of their skin. The tree gave them hope when they rubbed it. It gave them the chance of a wish come true, a dream fulfilled.

The visions Relly had when he touched each piece of wood were kind of like dreams. Each one a moment of moving pictures in his mind. Only, those visions had once taken place in real life.

"Can someone please tell us where we are going?" said April as they walked across the intersection. "It feels like we're going back the way we came."

"Here!" Relly said, stopping beside the real Tree of Hope.

"Here? Right here? We just left here." April crossed her arms. "Relly, we're going around in circles."

As they stood beside the tree again, Relly saw it in

a different light. Its trunk was a spine standing tall. Its branches stretched far out and above the street. Each branch seemed to try to tap each person who walked past. The tree wanted everyone's attention.

Relly pulled his backpack off for the zillionth time that day. There wasn't much in it, but each addition of wood had made the bag heavier on his shoulders and back. "This is how we get home."

"A tree?" Hudson asked, unconvinced.

"Not any tree," said Relly as he looked up, taking in the vastness. Relly pulled out the three pieces of wood. "This is Harlem's Tree of Hope. This is Harlem's wishing tree." Then Relly explained exactly what he had read in the book at the library.

"For years people have been coming to this tree to rub it for good luck. Some even made wishes before they went on to perform at a show. Performers, like my grandpa, would touch it, and when they performed, the tree brought them success. Kinda think of it as a tradition, or ritual, a good-luck charm that grows out of the ground."

"Like the Legacy Robe ceremony?" April said, referring to the Broadway tradition of a performer wearing a production's robe before the first show.

"So what does this tree have to do with getting us home?" Hudson asked. Relly inhaled. He knew the story of seeing visions at the bodega would sound unbelievable. But his friends still believed Relly when he told them. Relly touched the tree. He hoped they would believe his theory on how to get home, too.

"Here's my idea. I think these pieces of wood came from this exact tree."

Hudson tilted his head and raised an eyebrow. Relly continued.

"Promise I can explain. See?" Relly held up each piece. All three were spread in the palm of his hand. "The texture and colors match up." Relly held them closer to the tree. "You see how one side has bark and the other is smooth?" Relly asked. Monica nodded. April shrugged. Hudson only looked, still unconvinced. The sun had started to set. Relly would have to be fast.

"Here's my theory: I think each piece is a wish or hope that my grandpa once had. When the pieces were cut, the wishes and hopes were cut, too."

"That's what caused your Grandpa Gregory to doubt his own path as a tap dancer?" asked Monica.

"If we put them back, Grandpa gets his dreams back," said Relly. "That's my guess."

"And how is this going to get us home?" asked April.

Relly beamed. He thought he knew the exact way they could get home.

"We find where the pieces go. We put them back. Grandpa Gregory gets his motivation, and I think a path for us to get home will open. Then, bam, we're back in time for our own show, and Hudson won't ghost Selena Gomez for the next episode of FoodTube."

"Hudson, what do you think?" asked Monica.

"Best plan we've had all day!" Finally, Hudson looked as if he believed Relly. Hudson jumped forward, searching for holes in the tree. April, Monica, and Relly followed. They walked left to right, right to left, around the perimeter of the tree. But all they saw was bark. Then Relly started to look at each branch, but when he looked up, he realized the branches went from thick to thin.

"No way I can climb all the way to the top. Those limbs won't hold." *What if I'm wrong about the tree?* Relly thought. Relly needed to get his friends home. *This has to work!* He also needed his grandfather to get his motivation back. *Please let me be right.*

"Unless!" Relly shouted as he bent low, down to the base of the tree. "Unless it's not up; it's down."

The rest of the Squad did the same, bending low in search of three missing spots from Harlem's Tree of Hope. As Relly held each piece in his hand, they began to warm. Then his hand began to tingle. It started to stretch up the length of his arm, but right when he thought he would see yet another vision, he spotted them! Three identical carved-out slices of tree. Relly grabbed the first piece and lined it up with the hole. It looked as if it would fit. He began to bring it closer, ready to put the piece of wood back where it came from, back where it belonged. Then Relly stopped.

"What's wrong?" Monica asked as Relly held out the three pieces to his friends. "We're so close!"

"I know you can't see what I see, and there's nothing I can do about that. But it wouldn't be fair if I didn't let you match the pieces up where they belong. I'm the one who got us stuck in the fifties. I'm the one who called each of you down into the sewer. I'm the one who went to Shubert Alley instead of Al Joseph's when all April wanted was to grab a bite of food. And all Monica wanted was for us to have a sleepover. Now we're stuck in this together, and I want to get you home. You three can put the pieces back."

Hudson whispered a quiet "You sure?" Relly nodded. He was more than sure. Relly was positive.

April, Monica, and Hudson held their sliver of wood and bent low. They lined each one up to its empty spot, along the base of the tree. They lifted their pieces of wood and placed them back where they belonged, into the Tree of Hope. April, Monica, and Hudson pressed until each one fit in place.

Then the Squad stood back and waited. Hudson wiped

slivers of wood from his hands. Monica's eyes drooped, moving from hopeful to anxious. April bounced on the balls of her feet. For the first time in almost five months, Relly was shocked April did not have a single word to say.

"Nothing is happening," Monica noticed, letting her shoulders droop.

"What's supposed to happen?" Hudson asked.

"I . . . I don't know," Relly said. What *was* supposed to happen? Relly hoped the tree would physically change. Maybe glow where the pieces of wood were placed. Or illuminate a path for the Squad to take. Or shout, "Winner, winner, chicken dinner!" Instead, he saw nothing. The tree did not glow or light up a path. It did not shout or give a single answer on how to get home.

"Maybe they weren't the right pieces," said Monica.

"But they fit!" April shouted. "Exactly like a puzzle! Did you see when I fit mine? I literally heard it click in place. No way these aren't the right pieces. I mean, look at it." April waved her hands in front of where they had each placed the pieces of wood.

"Maybe we waited too late," Relly said. "It was a good try, just not the right one."

"So we really are stuck, huh?" asked Monica. "Ay, Dios mío!"

"No," said Relly. He knew his friends wanted to help. He

also knew they wanted to get home. Relly couldn't help but feel guilt at the excitement that had lit up their faces less than five minutes ago. That excitement was slowly replaced with disappointment. He barely wanted to even look at the Squad. He had gotten their hopes up, and his too.

"You should go back to Midtown, get back to the sewer, and see if you can pull the cover up. Then find a way out from there."

"Huh?" asked Hudson. "All the way back to Midtown?"

"But you're coming with us, right?" asked Monica.

"We're not going to leave you here," said April.

"I'll meet you in Shubert Alley," said Relly. "Later. Promise."

"We're a Squad, which means we don't leave someone behind just because an idea doesn't work," Monica said, but Relly only shrugged. "When will you meet us back in Shubert Alley?" Monica asked. Relly didn't know. He only hoped it would be soon.

"So what, the tree idea didn't work. We'll figure out another idea. There has to be a dozen ways for us to get home, right, Relly?" asked Hudson.

"To be honest, I've felt like Cinderella trying to beat the clock, except midnight is really seven thirty." April looked at the nearby clock tower. "We only have forty minutes left. I don't have a glass slipper, but I don't want to be turned into a pumpkin if we don't make it home in time."

"We can't leave you, Relly," said Monica, but Relly was already easing away. He began to walk faster up the street, farther away from his friends.

"It's fine!" Relly said, speeding up his walk until it became a swift run. "I'll see you in a few."

His friends still lingered beside the Tree of Hope until they finally understood Relly would not take no for an answer. April, Monica, and Hudson began to walk toward the subway station. Relly ran in the opposite direction.

Thirteen

7:15 P.M.

Forty-five minutes until Our Time

Evening began to fall over Harlem. There was now a deeper blanket of orange across the sky. Relly could feel the air cool each additional second he stayed in the past. When a streetlamp popped on, Relly knew seven thirty was approaching, and quick.

Relly walked past the Lafayette, away from the Tree of Hope, away from Harlem's Boulevard of Dreams. Now, on the next block, instead of theaters and restaurants and booming businesses, this street held houses. Tall brownstones with tall stairs and quaint stoops. Brownstones with arched windows and rectangular flower boxes. There weren't many people out on the sidewalks that night. For the first time since Relly had been in the past, he felt alone.

Relly Button?

The sound of Miss Sandra's voice filled Relly's mind as he walked. "Relly Button" was the name she used to call him. Each time he heard the nickname, it made him feel warm inside, like drinking a hot cup of Momma's cocoa.

Miss Sandra lived on the first floor, directly above the Mortons. When Momma started to work at the diner, Miss Sandra brought Relly to her dance studio. After school. Before school. Sometimes even during school on days when Relly said he was sick, but she knew he was pretending. Miss Sandra saw Relly dance one day and knew he was a natural.

She had a knack for asking Relly, "What's the matter?" She could always tell when Relly felt or looked as if the world had balanced itself and every single one of its problems on top of his shoulders.

Breathe, honey. Let that air fill your veins, and breathe.

As Relly walked, he noticed he had been holding his breath. Relly closed his eyes and grabbed hold of a nearby stoop rail. He stopped to steady his heartbeat, to gain his breath. He held one hand up and placed it above his heart. Then Relly took one deep breath in. One deep exhale out. Miss Sandra had always reminded Relly, "When you feel your heartbeat, how can there be any problems?"

Relly didn't know where he was going, where he was walking, but his legs continued to carry him until he found himself walking toward home. When he turned toward the intersection for 119th Street, Relly's heart began to pound quick. The tune mimicked the opening number for *Our Time*. Relly felt as if he had gotten offstage from another sold-out performance.

Relly never felt nerves before going on stage. But at that moment, he felt a tension roll through his body, right as he turned into what should have been Vanderzee Heights. The nerves he felt came because in 1958, there was no Vanderzee Heights. There was no twenty-seven-story brick building. There was no home.

Only the skeleton of the building existed. Bricks were scattered in piles on the ground. Windows weren't yet placed and were stacked in neat piles on the concrete. Not a single door had been hung. Those were on the ground too.

The only solid piece of this Vanderzee Heights was the staircase with its stoop. Relly recognized at that moment that all the memories he had about home had not been created yet.

"Why didn't I just ask you, Grandpa?" Relly thought out loud. When Grandpa Gregory had sat on the couch, asking Relly to find a backup plan, Relly wondered why he hadn't prodded his grandfather with questions. Questions like,

"Why and what and who made you think giving up was an option?"

The sounds of Harlem made a noise and rhythm that mimicked music, but Relly was not in the mood to tap. As call time approached and he still didn't have a way home, Relly was in the mood to think. Relly knew he had to find his grandfather again, and he wouldn't stop until he got Grandpa Gregory to believe in himself. Relly sat and let his thoughts wrap around his mind, like the sounds of tap that always wrapped around his tap shoes.

> *Grandpa is*
> *a Harlem legend*
> *stuck in a trunk*
> *of his own mind.*
> *Doubt and fear wrapped up*
> *so tight*
> *Slyde doesn't know how*
> *to be Slyde.*
> *Grandpa is*
> *a Harlem legend*
> *who's forgotten his*
> *own worth.*
> *I am Relly*
> *his grandson,*

come to remind him
he's Slyde.

When the chime of a clock went off, Relly jumped. He'd lost track of time, wondering and thinking and daydreaming. "I'm going to find you again," Relly vowed. Even if there was a way home, he could not leave without seeing Slyde one more time.

Relly took off.

Fourteen

It began to pour. Giant drops of rain soaked Relly from the tip of his hair to the soles of his sneakers. The drops were first a sprinkle. Then the sprinkle turned into a damp wet. The damp wet created a mist in the air that hovered above the sidewalks. Then the mist created haze. The word "change" had followed Relly around ever since he had entered the bodega.

I can change this, Relly thought. *I can get Grandpa to not give up.* Relly set off down 119th Street. He counted each block he ran through—*121st. 125th. 128th. 132nd*—until he was close enough to the Lafayette that he could see and hear the buzz of the theater's lights. Relly turned left on 135th. There, on the curb beside the theater, was the Squad. They had waited for him.

Relly felt a downpour of relief, or maybe it was just the rain. April, Monica, and Hudson sat on the curb outside the Lafayette. Relly wanted to hug them and high-five them, fist-bump and elbow-tap. He hadn't expected them to stay. He'd expected the Squad to find a way home. The relief sent waves of water to Relly's eyes. He didn't let a drop fall, but he was so happy to see them that he could cry.

They didn't leave me stuck in the fifties all by myself!

"You came back! You came back! You came back!"

"We didn't go anywhere," said Hudson. "We walked to the subway station, but when we started down the subway steps, we stopped. I couldn't just leave you. Neither could April and Monica."

"Relly!" April yelled. She stretched out her arms and ran over to give him a hug. This hug was followed by Monica's hug, which was followed by Hudson's hug. All three Squad members hugged and squeezed Relly tight.

"When we came back, you were nowhere near the theater. We went to the library. We went past the Apollo. We went to the park. Then we walked up and down Lenox, but we couldn't find you anywhere," April said. Relly felt too squished.

"Okay, okay! That's enough hugs!"

"Sorry!" April jumped back.

"Thanks for waiting for me," Relly said.

"Where were you? It was like you disappeared. Or were in hiding. Or had an invisibility cloak. Or up and vanished, poof, into the air," April said. "Hashtag 'Relly went ghost.'"

"I went home."

"Home!" the Squad shouted.

"Not future home. Just home. Vanderzee. My apartment building. But nothing is there besides the steps and building supplies. Listen, I'm sorry."

"Sorry for what?" Monica asked.

"I'm sorry for not telling you about the bodega, and the vision, and how I was having doubts about dancing," Relly said to his friends. "I'm sorry that I didn't say something sooner when all of this first started. If I did, we could have had it all figured out by now."

"Well, I'm sorry I dropped my phone," April added. "That's the only reason why you had to go inside that manhole."

"No, it's not," said Relly. "Jimmy told me to go to the alley for answers. That's the only reason I even went to Shubert Alley. And if you are sorry you dropped your phone, I'm sorry I bumped into you," Relly continued.

"I'm sorry I didn't order more food at the café, because if I did, I wouldn't be craving a supreme pizza with extra cheese," said Hudson. "Or a turkey sandwich."

"I'm sorry I didn't notice that Lloyd was following us," said Monica.

"Yada yada yada! Stop with the apologies. Have you ever heard me apologize? No! Why? Because I say what I mean, I mean what I say. Jeez, kids these days. So sentimental."

Relly swiveled in the direction of the voice.

"Ethel Merman!" Monica shouted. Ethel Merman had been standing outside the Lafayette, listening in on their conversation. *Did she hear everything*? Now Relly saw Ethel was not alone. There was a person standing beside Ethel who looked exactly like young Jimmy Onions.

"What are you doing here?" Monica asked Ethel.

"I came to see Slyde. I always come to see Gregory when his shows are in Harlem. Never in my lifetime did I think he would cancel his own show." Ethel came closer. She waved at the theater behind her. "So here I am, and there the theater is, jam-packed. Thought I was set until I heard his show was called off. No Slyde sliding tonight."

"I need to find him," said Relly. "He told Lloyd that they were going home. Do you know where they live?

"Ah, home," said Ethel. "Some say that's where the heart is. For Slyde, home is where the hoof is."

"Whatcha saying?" Hudson asked.

"Hoofers," said Ethel.

"Hoofers?" repeated the Squad.

"It's the club," Ethel said, matter-of-factly. "Slyde and Lloyd don't live there, but Hoofers may as well be a second home for Slyde. So that's possibly what he meant. Most dancers go to Hoofers after their shows at the Lafayette. Hoofers Club has all the tap legends. What you need to look out for are the ones who steal steps."

"Steal steps?" asked Hudson.

"From tap dancers with chops."

"Chops?" Hudson asked.

"Skill. Talent. Charisma. Artistry. Prowess. All the exceptional artists of any art form steal from the ones who did it first. Then they make it look brand new, as if they made it up on their own."

"Where is Hoofers?" Relly asked.

"Round the corner," said Ethel. "Makes it easy to get to from the Lafayette."

The Squad, Ethel, and young Jimmy set out for the Hoofers Club.

Ethel was right, it really was around the corner. Because after the short five-minute walk, they all found themselves standing in front of a three-story, peculiar-looking brick building. A sound vibrated off the building's exterior. The sound fizzled out, not quite strong enough to make it to Relly's ears. Relly stepped forward, closer. He listened and homed in on the noise. Relly began to feel the sound in his feet. He wondered if the Squad could feel that sound too.

It was the sound of tap.

Jimmy pulled the door open, letting Ethel and the Squad step inside. The entrance opened to a lobby. Relly could tell people had been there recently. Except, at that moment, no one was in the lobby. The hardwood floor was scuffed up from shoes. Damp puddles coated the floor. Coats hung from hangers. People were in the building, lots of them. But not a single person was in eyesight. *Where were they now?*

The sound of laughter and clatter of talking crept up a single stairway beside the lobby door. When another person entered through the front doors, they immediately took the steps. They raced down three at a time. Relly knew the stairs had to be the real way to Hoofers.

The steps led to a landing that opened into one large hardwood-floored room. At the very front of the room was an elevated wooden stage. Relly measured it in his head. The room had to be as large as his apartment if the apartment had no walls. It was half the size of the Ethel Merman Theater's own stage.

"Why does it have that name?" Hudson asked Ethel.

"To be a hoofer, you feel and breathe in the sounds. Those sounds travel down to your soul. That's when you and only you will know to tap is to live." When Relly heard Ethel describe a hoofer, he knew he had been one his entire life.

"That sounds like poetry," Monica said.

"Oh, honey, it is poetry," said Ethel.

"Sounds like how I feel when I'm up on stage," replied April.

"Sounds like that feeling I get doing FoodTube," said Hudson.

"When ya know, ya know," Ethel responded.

Forks clanged against plates. Shoes tapped against wood. All the talking added to the clamor. The tables that were scattered about the room had some seats full, others not so much. People that were seated got up and started to dance.

The attire for the night seemed to be a mix-and-match of fancy sequined dresses with fancy sequined heels. Plain plaid dresses with even more plain Mary Janes shoes. Black suits and silk ties with sparkly shined loafers. Pants with suspenders and button-up shirts. No one seemed to pay any attention to the four kids with clothing that had not yet been made. The people were either too busy dancing in their seats, too busy dancing on the floor, or watching the next person up on stage. That next person was a kid named Hines.

The Hines kid tapped with a smile on his face and a cool, smooth ease to his moves. The moment reminded Relly of how he felt at home up on any stage.

"I need to find my grandpa," Relly tried to say over the noise, but the Squad hadn't heard him. Right then, a piano began to play. Music surrounded the room. It wasn't only a piano Relly saw; there was an entire band beside the stage. All types of instruments stood off to the side, and behind them were musicians. On the instruments was the name of a band.

"Cab Calloway?" Relly whispered as music erupted from the instruments. A man behind a microphone began to sing.

The jim, jam, jump on the jumpin' jive
Makes you like your eggs on the Jersey side
Hep-hep!

"Legendary," Hudson whispered back.

"You want us to help you, Relly?" Monica asked. "Help you find your grandfather?"

"Yeah, it'll take you forever to find him in this crowd," said Hudson as he reached for an appetizer being passed around on a tray.

"Ooh, bacon-stuffed mushrooms!"

"No, I need to do this on my own." Relly set off to find Grandpa Gregory. He squeezed between trays of appetizers held up on hands and people dancing in the middle of the floor. Someone did a spin and Relly did one too. From the back of the room to the front, then from the left side of the room to the right, Relly roamed, looking for Grandpa Gregory.

Even though the place was packed, it didn't take long for him to find the young version of his grandfather. Slyde sat in the very back corner of the room. If Relly had been walking a little too fast, maneuvering between people a little too swift, he would have missed his young grandfather. A shadow hung over the tap dancer. When Relly sat down, Slyde didn't even look up.

"You made wishes. You rubbed them in the tree."

"Say what, now?" Slyde shifted in his seat. He lifted his head to look at Relly.

"The first wish, you made when you were a kid. You wanted to dance instead of play the violin. The second wish, you made when you were my age. You wanted to learn how to slide. The third wish, you made when you were a little older. You wanted to be an extraordinary tap dancer. You made those wishes and rubbed them into the Tree of Hope."

"You're wasting your time, son," Slyde said. "Go home to your parents. You're wasting your breath trying to talk to me."

"What happened? Why did you carve out your wishes? Did all that doubt and fear creep up in you because you were scared? Want to know what I think? I think we have a choice. We can give up or we can follow our dreams. Either choice is yours." Relly thought he saw Lloyd peek from behind a person in the crowd.

"So what if I give up?"

"You'll regret it in the future."

"How do you know I'll regret anything?" Slyde asked.

"Because you'll take it out on those who love you. You'll take it out on people in the future, like me."

"Like you?" Slyde laughed. "Kid, I don't even know you."

"You will, when we meet again." Relly gulped. Maybe he shouldn't have said that, but it was too late now. Slyde could either take his words or he could leave them. Relly stood. He held out his hand, palm facing up. Slyde looked at Relly's hand, then looked Relly in the face. It took a moment before Slyde grabbed Relly's hand in a shake. Relly left the young version of his grandfather at the table.

When Relly rejoined the Squad, it was clear his friends were having the time of their lives. Relly took in the scene, the people, the dancing and singing. The comfort in the room oozed. But there was something else he needed to do. Relly slipped away from the Squad before Hudson, April, and Monica could even realize he had left again. Seeing the head peek out from behind yet another person, this time, Relly knew it was Lloyd.

"Hey!" Relly waved him over.

"Hay is for horses," Lloyd joked. All of a sudden, Relly's palms felt sweaty. But he wanted to talk to Lloyd. It was nice to spend time with him throughout the day. But it would be even nicer to have a real conversation with his younger dad.

"I'm . . . ," Relly began.

"You're different, you know that?" Lloyd asked. Relief swept over Relly. At least Lloyd was changing the subject.

"Who crawls out of sewers? Ha! You're an explorer, and a questioner, and an adventurer! I like it! Wanna know what I felt when I saw you and your friends coming out that sewer? I felt like I already knew you."

Relly felt a chill cool his body.

"Did it feel that way to you?"

"Yeah . . . that's exactly how it felt."

Lloyd didn't ask why Relly and his friends had come out of the sewer. He didn't ask where they had come from, either. Instead, Lloyd held out his hand and waited for Relly to do the same.

"I have a super-secretive handshake. It's one I only reserve for my friends."

"I thought you said you didn't have any friends."

"You'll be the first."

Relly held out his hand. The two joined their hands together. It was an up and a down, with a clap to the side. A clap in the air. The click of one thumb against a finger, then the other.

"Want me to show you mine?" Relly said after their handshake was finished. Relly showed Lloyd the up-and-down handshake that Relly reserved for his brother. Relly and Lloyd tapped their knuckles together. And as they did, Relly thought of all the things he wanted to do with his dad. All the things he hadn't been able to do since he was three, he had done them on that day.

Relly had one more meal with his dad. One more train ride to Harlem. Relly was able to speak to his dad again, and this time, his dad answered. But Relly still didn't know if his dad would ever see him perform.

Relly's eyes darted to the stage. One performer had stepped off, finishing his segment. He grabbed a glass of water from the edge of the stage. Then, as he walked across the platform to exit, the water overflowed from the rim of the glass. It splashed on the stage floor. When it hit the floor, the water spread. The crowd erupted into a mixture of claps and shouts, paying no attention to the water on the floor. But Relly kept looking. It was time for the next performer to take the stage at Hoofers.

That next performer was Slyde.

Grandpa! Relly thought as he watched Slyde ease his way through the crowd, then up the few steps on the side of the stage. Finally, his talk with his younger grandfather had paid off. But Slyde was unaware of the water on the floor. Water that would surely make him fall if he were to slide and glide. So much for a signature move. Relly slipped himself between person after person, rushing his way to the front of the stage.

"Stop!" Relly yelled, still eyeing the water on the floor. "Stop!"

"Are you trying to ruin me?" Slyde asked Relly.

"No, I'm trying to help you. Anyone have a mop?"

"A mop!" someone yelled from the crowd.

"What's the kid want with a mop?" someone else asked. "Never seen anybody tap dance with a mop!" But by then, a mop had been handed to Relly.

"Sorry, Grandpa," Relly said.

"Gran-who?" asked Slyde.

"This will only take a second." Relly quickly soaked up the water on the floor. Three quick swipes across the hard-wood stage.

"The floor is yours." Relly jumped down, eager to escape Slyde asking why Relly had called him Grandpa. As the noise of the crowd settled, the band picked up once again. And Slyde began to tap. Steps that started off cool and smooth. With a brush of his heel, then the brush back, and a shuffle to the side. Slyde's left foot took off. He completed this tap move with another simple ball change before going into a set of back-and-forth slides.

Then, Slyde waved his hand for Relly to join him. Relly didn't hesitate to hop onstage. Each time Slyde stepped back, Relly stepped forward. When Relly stepped back, Slyde stepped forward. Both eased into a natural rhythm, letting each other take turns in the spotlight of the stage. Relly knew what was coming up next: Slyde's signature move. The grand finale. But when Relly looked down, Hudson, April, and Monica were looking up at him, frantic.

"We only have fifteen minutes!" Hudson yelled.

"Fifteen minutes?" Relly repeated.

"We have to leave now!" April said as Monica gave Relly a look of sympathy.

With Slyde on the opposite end of the stage, Relly saw he was ready to take off in his signature move. The slide.

At that moment, Relly jumped down onto the hardwood floor below. He slipped through the crowd, rushing to catch up with Monica, April, and Hudson. As his friends left the room and started to climb the steps, Relly did not look back.

"Sorry, Grandpa," Relly whispered as he ran up the steps. Behind him, Relly heard the crowd cheer.

Fifteen

Fifteen minutes until Our Time

When they reached the lobby doors Relly pushed them open. As he stepped outside, he expected to be hit by a downfall of rain, but the rain had finally stopped. The sound of people dancing and tapping inside Hoofers Club echoed outside as the Squad reached the sidewalk.

"What next?" Hudson asked.

"We need to make it to Midtown," Monica said. "And back to our present."

"Before the start of our show? That's impossible," April said. "It's seven forty-five right now. We go on in fifteen!"

It sounded impossible to Relly, too. "What subway do you

know that will get us from Harlem to Midtown to the present in less than fifteen minutes?"

"None," Relly, Hudson, and Monica said. By now, they moved between a walk and a run. Up the street, past Hoofers, away from the building that echoed sounds of tap. Then they made a left on 132nd Street. The Lafayette with its bold lights was up ahead. The light against the tree gave the towering timber a serene look. The tree looked deep in thought.

"This is the wrong way," April said. But Relly felt the urge to keep going forward, toward the theater. Closer to the Tree of Hope.

"Relly, did you hear me? I said this is the wrong way."

"I know, I know!" said Relly. "But maybe we missed something. Maybe there are more than three clues, and we haven't found them all yet. Or maybe I was the one who should have put the pieces of wood in place. Or Grandpa?"

"Well, if there are more pieces, they'll have to stay lost!" Hudson exclaimed. "Our time is almost gone, Relly."

"And what if nothing is missing?" said April. "You found the three pieces, they just didn't do anything."

The Squad found themselves beside Harlem's Tree of Hope, back where they had been over an hour ago. The pieces of wood were still at the base of the tree. But, like earlier, there was no indication that this tree would change and give them a way to get home. Relly looked up. The tree towered above him. His eyes reached to the tallest branch.

Relly held his breath. He closed his eyes and reached out to touch the trunk of the tree.

"Please let us find a way home," Relly said, rubbing the tree trunk with his hand. When Relly opened his eyes, he saw Monica, April, and Hudson had done the same. Their eyes were closed and arms outstretched, making a wish.

A block ahead, Relly saw the outline of a man and child running toward the Squad. Against the concrete side-walk, Relly could hear a *tap, tap, tap. Clank, clank, clank.* Someone was running in tap shoes.

"Grandpa!" Relly shouted. "I mean, Slyde!"

Slyde and Lloyd reached the Squad. Lloyd placed his hands on his knees, trying to catch his breath. "Hey! You left without saying goodbye."

"We're kind of in a rush," said Hudson.

"Yeah, but there's always time to say goodbye," said Lloyd, looking up at Relly.

"My son is right," Slyde said.

"I wanted to thank you before you wandered off. You missed the best part of the show."

"Thank me for what?"

"For not giving up on me. For pushing some belief back

into my stubborn head. I was on the verge of giving up my own dream." Slyde touched his hand to the tree for balance, palm against the Tree of Hope. "Thank you," said Slyde, "for believing in me."

Right when Relly was about to let it all loose, right when he was about to spill where he was from and exactly who Slyde was to Relly, the tree moved. Relly felt the shake of each branch and leaf up above. The tree trunk vibrated against the palm of Slyde's hand. Relly and the Squad looked down at the places where they had inserted the three slivers of wood earlier.

"Relly, you were right," Hudson said. "Look!" The spots where the three pieces were placed now glowed. It was a moonlight beaming off the ocean–type glow. It was an early-morning-sunrise-across-Harlem-type glow. Then the glowing stopped. The shaking stopped. The tree was back to being still and quiet and serene. Slyde removed his hand as if nothing had ever even happened. April turned toward the street. She beckoned the Squad to do that same, then she pointed to the middle of Seventh Avenue, where a sewer hole had opened. It glowed too.

"Welp, I'm out. See ya when I see ya. Bye to the bye to the bye. That's our way home and I'm taking no chances of that thing closing up," Hudson said. "You wanna stay in the fifties? Be my guest." Hudson looked both ways before he ran out into the street and approached the glowing sewer.

"So dramatic," said April as she followed him. Monica glowed against the light. "We're getting home!" she whispered to Relly before joining April and Hudson.

Relly noticed Slyde bending low to the tree stump. He raised his arm and ran his hand against the base of the tree. Slyde stood again, looking at Relly.

"You were right. I was the one who cut out pieces of this tree. When I thought my dreams of becoming a tap dancer would never come true, I left home late one night and carved out each piece. I was so angry. You know how it feels to see folks around you reaching their dreams?"

Relly nodded. That's how it felt sometimes when he was around Bobby. Grandpa Gregory gave Bobby plenty of praise for wanting to be an engineer.

"Everyone in Harlem says this tree brings luck. Everyone says to touch it and watch your wish come true. I did exactly that. I waited and waited. But nothing. Seeing everyone else around me have fame and success, I just could not wait any longer. So I gave up and took my wishes back. A choice, I know. But it was my choice."

Lloyd stepped forward. He looked up at Slyde with his large, round eyes.

"That's not all, Dad," said Lloyd. "'Cause I found them."

"Found what?" Relly asked.

"Two minutes, Relly!" Monica shouted from beside the sewer.

"The pieces from the tree my dad cut! I found them in his coat pocket back at home a few months ago."

"Relly!" shouted April.

"I didn't like how down in the dumps my dad was. Every single day he was moping over those wishes that didn't come true. So I scattered them around the city. I thought I was helping. I just didn't want Dad to hurt."

Slyde nudged Lloyd back up the sidewalk.

"Thank you for putting my wishes back," said Slyde as they waved goodbye. Relly swallowed the knot that had grown in his chest. As Relly joined April, Monica, and Hudson at the sewer, he turned around, watching Slyde and Lloyd leave. The sound of Slyde's shoes got more faint the farther they walked. Relly missed Lloyd already.

The sewer glowed light yellow. Relly compared it to the waterfall onstage during *Our Time*. Only this glow wasn't water. It was a glow of light that erupted over their heads as they stood at the edge of the sewer. The light swirled, but it did not touch them. Then the waterfall of light stretched and reached up until it met with the sky. The sewer hole brightened until Relly saw a ladder.

"This is our way out," Relly said, taking the first step down. With no hesitation, the rest of the Squad descended into the hole behind him.

"What was that?" Hudson asked, a few ladder rungs above.

"I don't know, but put the cover back!" Relly shouted from the bottom of the sewer. He saw Hudson slide the cover back in place. Then April, Monica, and Hudson scrambled to the bottom of the sewer after Relly. The Squad was safe as a rattling came from up above. The glow of the light began to fade.

"I think the fifties are ending," said Relly. "Well, our time in the fifties." Relly pushed the door open. He expected to see the posters and graffiti that lined up the sewer walls. Instead, when he opened the door and stepped out into the other side, there was nothing. Even the wet yuck was gone. The sewer was dry, void of any images and words on the wall.

"This doesn't look like the way we came," said Hudson.

"Because it's not," said Relly. "But it opened for us, so this is the way we're going home."

The Squad wasted no more time in the sewer. They walked, then ran, ducking their heads under beams and squeezing between tight corners when the sewer twisted and turned. Relly felt he had been in the sewer for hours.

Relief flooded the Squad when they finally found another ladder. The Squad shouted, happy to have found a way out. Hudson ran ahead. He was the first to climb up the ladder rungs.

Hudson was followed by April. April was followed by Monica. Monica was followed by Relly. All three climbed and waited as Hudson lifted the heavy cover up above. Relly could hear people walking across the pavement overhead.

The moment Relly's hands touched the pavement, he hoisted himself up. He looked out toward each building. There, across the way, were the Shubert and Booth theaters. Each theater had marquees and each marquee scrolled the names of shows in bright, multicolored lights. The Squad was not in 1958 anymore. They were back in *their* time. *Their* Shubert Alley.

There was one thing that Relly wished hadn't changed. When Relly finally exited the sewer, he had an inkling he would see Lloyd. But when he looked up ahead, to where the poster of *Peter Pan* should have been, there was no younger version of his dad.

Once the rest of the Squad exited, Relly slid the cover back. A vibration came from his backpack. Then came the noise. Each of their phones sounded off. Four different ringtones for four different devices. April's ringtone chimed "A Whole New World."

"I'm like a shooting star. I've come so far!" April sung along. The last time Relly had seen his friends this relieved was when they solved the curse of the Ethel Merman Theater.

Relly's phone sounded off too. It was a combination, a syncopation of tunes from the musician Jelly Roll. Relly opened his backpack, handing his friends their phones. He unlocked his phone and stared down as a series of text messages popped up.

Bobby: We're on our way! Momma wants 2 know how the slumber party went.

Momma: Wait until you see your grandpa!

Momma: . . . Hello? I know you got my text, Relly. Hello?

Bobby: Aye! You backstage? Someone named Claudia Middleton is looking for you.

Claudia Middleton.

"We've got to go now!" Relly shouted. He looked down at his phone again, this time to check the time. It had been close to eight o'clock when they entered the sewer from Harlem. He glanced at his phone: 7:29. One minute until call time. Passing through the sewer had somehow pushed back time. Thank goodness, or thank the Tree of Hope, they still had a whole ten minutes before they would be considered late.

Sixteen

THE SOUND OF HARLEM
Half hour till showtime

As the Squad left the alley, they ran to the Ethel Merman Theater. Relly wondered how anyone walking up and down the middle of New York City wasn't gawking in shock over four kids who were once stuck in the fifties. He wondered how the people waiting outside the theater weren't standing wide-eyed and open-mouthed at four kids who just stepped out of a different decade. The shock of what they had been through finally hit Relly. He knew the amount of luck it had taken for them to figure out a way back home. A way back before showtime. Some serious luck.

The stage door popped open as the Squad approached.

Jimmy stepped outside the Ethel Merman Theater. He must have watched them approach on his surveillance camera. He held the door open for the Squad to enter.

"Hey, Jimmy!" April said, giving the doorman a hug. April pulled out her phone and tapped the screen. She tapped to the camera and snapped a quick selfie of her and the doorman.

"Hashtag 'best doorman ever'! Hashtag 'it's good to be back'!" April said as she made a new post. "Hashtag 'huge sigh of relief'!"

Jimmy nodded at Relly, Monica, and Hudson as he shut the stage door. He eyed them as they walked through; then he sat down at the table, humming his same tune.

"I thought I'd never see this place again!" April shouted, grabbing a dry-erase marker and scribbling her initials on the call-board.

"You can say that again," said Hudson, also scribbling down his initials.

"I thought I'd never see this place!"

Relly and Monica signed their initials too. Relly made sure to trace his twice. He went over the *R. L. M.* with the black dry-erase marker. He pressed down hard over each letter. He did not want to take any chances with Claudia doubting if he was on time.

"Everything is the same," Monica whispered to Relly,

April, and Hudson. She glanced around the hallway. Relly agreed. Same names on the call-board, same magic tricks and joke books on the shelf beside Jimmy's table. Same Jimmy.

"Got a missed call from my little sister," said April. "And a call from my mom, and a text from my dad. They are all annoyed they couldn't see me before our show. They haven't changed either."

Relly thought he heard the Squad take a collective sigh of relief.

"My abuelita left me a message. Said she made two whole trays of cookies. Hudson, they are all yours," Monica said. The Squad watched as Hudson jumped up on the balls of his feet.

"Yippee! Cookies!"

"Was your abuelita freaking out that we didn't show up at your house for our sleepover?" April asked.

"Nope!" Monica shook her head. "Before we headed down the ladder to the sewer, I sent her a text. Told her we were sleeping over at your house last night."

"My house?"

"Yep. Figured things might take a while."

"Relly?" Jimmy said as Relly capped the marker.

"Yup?" Relly replied. April, Monica, and Hudson were already walking up the stairs, headed to their dressing rooms to change. But before Jimmy could get his words out, Relly said his.

"Why did you tell me to go to the alley?" asked Relly. He saw Jimmy had been working on a wildlife puzzle that covered the entire width of the table. It was a puzzle of a moose beside a pond. Five hundred pieces and Jimmy only had a handful left to place.

"Wild guess," Jimmy said, securing a piece of the moose's antlers. "That's where I go when I need to clear my mind. Figured it would do the same for you."

Relly raised an eyebrow as Jimmy removed a piece that didn't quite fit. Then Jimmy held another puzzle piece up for inspection. He waved it around the table, finding the correct spot. Finally, Jimmy put that piece down. It snapped into place.

"Well, did it, Relly? Did the alley help clear your head?"

"You coming, Relly?" Hudson yelled down the stairs.

"In a second!" Relly yelled back. He stared at Jimmy, then stared at the puzzle, then stared at Jimmy again. "Something like that," said Relly.

"Relly L. Morton, if you are in the building, let me know," a voice came over the speakers. "This is Claudia. See me backstage—please!"

"Thanks," Relly said, holding out his fist.

"Anytime, kiddo," Jimmy said as both their fists bumped.

Then Relly ran up the stairs and headed backstage.

A faint murmur of people in seats and people walking up and down the aisles escaped beneath the stage curtain. It was the noise of school groups trying to find their correct seats. And people who were already seated getting up to let others pass through. When Relly approached backstage, the lights overhead were bright. A member of the stage crew pushed a long sweeper across the stage. It was one final attempt at cleaning up and making sure the set was dust-free as another stage crew tidied the living room scene. The living room was the first scene in *Our Time.*

Relly didn't see Claudia at first. Then he heard her shoes walk across the stage. The sound was headed in his direction. Claudia stopped when she saw Relly. At first, there was a look of disappointment on her face. Then the look turned quick, replaced with glee. Claudia yelped.

"There you are!" Claudia held out her hands to give Relly a hug. Relly stood onstage, frozen. How was he supposed to react? Wasn't Claudia the one saying she would kick him out of the show on his third strike? Now she wants to give him a hug like he's a long-lost survivor come back from a desert island.

"Have you seen your understudy, Jacob, yet?"

Jacob?

"No." Relly shook his head as Claudia stepped back. "Why would I have seen Jacob?"

"Oh! He just loves you, Relly. Said he wanted to have a word. Told me to tell you to break a leg, do your thing. Break both legs, for that matter! Ha! Isn't Jacob funny? He knows this is a big night for you. He said, and I quote, 'Could not imagine a more perfect fit for Pax besides Relly L. Morton.'"

Relly just stared. "He said that?"

"Of course he said that!"

"Are you serious?"

"Of course I'm serious!"

"Jacob? Understudy Jacob? Jacob, who listens to seagull sounds to get into the correct headspace before going onstage? That Jacob?"

Claudia pulled out her notebook and flipped it open. She pulled a pen from her pocket and checked off a page of notes. "If I don't check it off, I'll forget," Claudia said, pocketing the notebook and pen again. "My brain is always so scattered. My mother used to say my brain is cluttered, but I beg to differ. I just like to think . . . a lot. Anyhoo, that's not why I called you here, Relly. You know why I called you backstage?"

"So you can kick me out of the show?" That was Relly's only guess. "I wasn't late today. You can check the call-board. You can ask Jimmy. You can ask Monica, April, and Hudson too. We got back around seven thirty, which means I don't have much time to get dressed, but I was not late!"

"NO!" Claudia looked horrified. "What? I have never made note of you being late. You can look in my notebook. Tardiness happens. Trains happen. Life happens. You know me, I'll give you plenty of chances; that's Claudia Middleton."

"You've never marked me as late?" Relly asked.

"Never."

"Ever?"

Claudia shook her head. This was news to Relly.

"Then why did you call me here?" Relly asked.

"We have a special guest. I wanted you to know before the start of show."

"Really? Who?"

"Oh, you know our guest," Claudia said as a man in a gray suit with a headful of gray hair stepped onto the stage. He walked in from the wing with a smooth, cool ease, toward the middle of the stage, where Relly and Claudia stood. The man in his nineties took long strides across the floor as he reached them both.

"Grandpa?" Relly asked. Grandpa Gregory could have stepped out of a movie. He looked good! Relly had never seen his grandfather walk with such elegance. Such grace. So confidently. Normally, Grandpa Gregory was stuck on the couch, muscles aching, and complaining. But now, he didn't even need a walker or a cane.

"What are you doing here?" Relly asked, looking from the stage curtain back to his grandfather. "Don't you need to find your seat?"

"Relly Rel. My man." Grandpa Gregory wrapped his arms around his grandson. Grandpa Gregory squeezed Relly so tight, it felt like the hug Relly had given his grandfather in the fifties.

"You look great," Relly said. "I've never seen you walk so free before."

"Say what, now, Grandson? You know me. I'm always on my feet. Never been off my feet. Had a close call once about sixty-four years ago with some water on a stage. Now, if I had slipped and fell, my career would have been over."

"It worked, then," said Relly. Even mopping up the water at Hoofers Club had helped Grandpa Gregory.

"What worked, son?" Grandpa Gregory asked, taking a step back to get a good look at Relly.

"Nothing! Oh, nothing! What are you doing here?"

Grandpa Gregory laughed. "The other night when I was half asleep on the couch, you said you would ask your stage manager if I could be a special guest during tonight's show. You said it would be your birthday gift to me. Well, what I didn't tell you was it would be my honor, my gift for the cast, the crew, the audience. Not often I get to perform like I used to."

"Huh? I said that?" Relly asked. Then he picked up on what else his grandfather said. "Like you used to? What do you mean?"

"They don't call me Slyde for nothing!"

"Mr. Gregory 'Slyde' Morton is a phenomenon," Claudia said. "Not that either of you need reminding of that!" Claudia stepped forward to shake Slyde's hand. "I just love your origin story, Mr. 'Slyde' Morton. How you were found by a scout at Hoofers Club one night in the fifties. How that night changed the entire course of your career. So classic. So original." Claudia looked down at her watch. Relly peeped Hudson, April, and Monica in a wing of the stage. They were fully dressed in their characters' costumes. Relly was the only one still not ready.

"Um, you are performing tonight, right?" Hudson asked.

"Yep!" Relly said. He had less than ten minutes to get dressed. But he had gotten ready in less time than that before. No biggie.

"I'll see you after the show, Grandpa," Relly said, running past the wing, then down a hall. When Relly finally turned to his dressing room, he let out a breath of relief.

Curtain.

As the closing music for *Our Time* echoed through the Ethel Merman Theater, the ensemble grabbed hold of each other's hands. The entire cast formed one long strand of people and bowed in unison as the audience rumbled with claps and whoops. Foot stomps and hollers. The audience's cheers were a compliment to a show well done. The ensemble for *Our Time* bowed again, then held their hands out toward the orchestra pit. Relly knew there would be no show without the orchestra.

Relly was the first to step forward out of the Squad. He was followed by Monica, who was followed by April, and then Hudson. Again, they gripped hands and bowed. The audience's claps erupted even louder as Relly peeked down below. There was his family, Momma, Bobby, and Grandpa Gregory, sitting in the front row. As the claps quieted, Monica, April, and Hudson went back to join the ensemble. Relly stood in the spotlight, downstage, in the center.

When Relly looked out to his family, Grandpa Gregory beamed. Out of all the shows he had performed, Relly rarely felt nervous. But in feeling Grandpa Gregory smile up at him, all at once, Relly's heartbeat pounded fast. By now, the orchestra had quieted their closing music.

Right when Relly was about to say a few words, he watched as Claudia Middleton walked past the front row of seats. She stopped at Grandpa Gregory and whispered into his ear. Then Grandpa Gregory got up and followed Claudia. Through the front row, down the side aisle, and out the exit next to the stage. A few seconds later, Grandpa Gregory approached Relly from stage right. When he got closer, Relly embraced him in a tight hug. Then, turning to the audience, Relly knew exactly what he wanted to say.

"You've probably heard of Slyde," Relly began to tell the audience. "Maybe you know him as a tap-dancing legend out of Harlem. But to me, Slyde is Grandpa. Grandpa Gregory used to tap at a place in Harlem, a theater that's not there anymore. He's got a signature move called the slide . . ." Relly did a quick and short slide as Grandpa Gregory let out a laugh.

"Bet all the tap dancers have tried to copy Grandpa's moves. But no one can slide like Slyde." Relly turned to Grandpa Gregory. "Grandpa, some days I might not show it, but I want you to know you're my inspiration. When none of us are sure what step to take next, you keep moving. That means I'll keep moving too."

Now Grandpa gave Relly an even tighter hug as the audience erupted into claps and cheers. The orchestra picked up their music as Grandpa Gregory's and Relly's feet began to move. In sync with the orchestra beat, even though Grandpa didn't have on tap shoes, his feet hit up against the stage floor in a series of steps. Front then back. Back then front. A pause and Grandpa Gregory turned, doing a full spin.

"I got you beat!" Relly said, and the audience's cheers echoed even louder. Relly joined in with Grandpa Gregory's moves, until he found himself sliding. The two took off in a short slide stage left. Then they moved their feet, tapping until they each slid on one leg. Going the opposite direction, they repeated the move, sliding until they reached stage right.

Grandpa Gregory did one more spin and Relly followed his grandfather's move until the two grabbed hands and bowed. Just like back at Hoofers in 1958, the audience cheered.

On the subway ride from Midtown to Harlem, Relly thought about how Grandpa Gregory's life was altered because Relly helped him to not give up. The only other thing Relly wanted was to have his dad back forever. When Momma opened the apartment door, the family stepped inside. Relly held out a tiny bit of hope he would see his dad.

He will be here, Relly thought, closing his eyes. Not as a kid, as a parent. Relly pictured his dad fixing the leaky faucet in the bathroom. Or fixing the broken coffeepot in the kitchen. He pictured his father looking up and smiling as the family walked in, ready to give Relly his signature handshake. But when Relly opened his eyes, it was still only the four of them inside of the tiny apartment. For a moment, his heart felt as if it were being squeezed by a dozen secret handshakes.

Bobby and Relly slipped off their shoes as Grandpa Gregory slid his coat onto the rack beside the front door. Momma headed for the kitchen table, which Relly saw was set with plates, forks, and glasses.

"I owe you an apology," Bobby said, placing his shoes on top of the shoe rack.

"For what?" Relly asked, doing the same.

"For being tough on you the other day at the bodega."

"It's nothing," said Relly. He had almost forgotten how annoyed Bobby was only a few days ago.

"I made a feast for Grandpa's birthday, and it's my cooking, not the diner's. Come eat before it gets cold," said Momma. "I will not let my hard work go to waste." When the family moved into the kitchen, they saw Momma's feast.

"There's cheesy lasagna and asparagus. Garlic bread and salad. I made that pineapple upside-down cake from scratch!" *Happy Birthday, Grandpa Gregory!* was written on a card in gold ink next to the cake.

"Don't say it's nothing, Relly," said Bobby. "Some days I'm the annoying older brother treating you like you are still a little kid. But you've got the whole neighborhood and all of Broadway giving you props. I act like you need someone to hold your hand. You're more than capable, Relly. Aye, you're the one who got yourself a role in a Broadway show. You know who you are. You know what you want. And I need to learn how to step back and watch you grow."

Relly sat down at the table, next to Grandpa Gregory.

"Are you still going to find me some engineering workshop to take?" Relly asked, ignoring the concerned look on his grandfather's face. Bobby held up his hands. He moved them together, shifting them back and forth, as if he were rubbing an invisible paper towel.

"Engineering? Nope. You don't need them. You already know you're a star."

"My grandson better not give up tap."

Momma scooped lasagna on her plate. Relly caught her glance at Bobby and nod. Even Grandpa mumbled a few "Uh-huh"s and "That's right" after Bobby's words. Relly passed the bread to Grandpa. Momma passed the asparagus to Bobby. Relly kept quiet, taking a bite of salad. He waited to hear if Bobby had more to say.

"So that's why I'm not going to meet you after your shows anymore."

"What!" Relly hollered.

"Relly L. Morton! Keep your voice down. It's late," Momma said. The walls in the apartment were thin, and their upstairs neighbors were sleeping.

"Well, why not?" Relly asked.

Bobby took a bite of lasagna. "You're old enough now to come home by yourself, whether it's dark or not. I trust you. Momma trusts you. Grandpa trusts you. You can't be almost thirteen and still have your older brother follow you around New York. How's that going to look?"

Relly had gotten used to his brother showing up after his shows to take him home. But Bobby was right. If Relly had traversed almost all of New York City with only his friends, he was more than capable of coming home by himself after a late show.

After the family ate, Relly lit the candles on Grandpa's birthday cake. The family sang two versions of "Happy Birthday" to Grandpa Gregory. The first was the regular version everyone sang whether someone was turning ninety-five or seven. The second song was the version by Stevie Wonder, one of Momma's favorite singers. Momma nudged Relly.

"Want me to play it from my phone?" he asked.

"Give us some background music," Momma said. Relly typed in the song title, then he let the tune play. Momma stood and started to dance. She swayed to the beat, snapping her fingers and moving her shoulders. Momma started singing in the middle of the kitchen floor.

"Happy birthday to ya! Happy birthdayyy!" Relly, Bobby, and Momma sung as Grandpa Gregory got up and did a slide. He slid from the sink to the table. Then he slid from the hallway to the couch. Bobby tried to mimic Grandpa, only Bobby's moves were two inches too short. This made the whole family burst out laughing.

When the family went to eat Grandpa's cake, Relly watched as Grandpa Gregory took a bite. If Relly looked hard, he could young Grandpa. Young Slyde. The remnant of the man his grandfather had been in the fifties.

Relly smiled; then he thought about the rooftop. If there was any place for his grandfather to slide, it would be on the roof of Vanderzee Heights. It would be for all of Harlem to hear. For the stars and maybe Lloyd to peek.

"I need to show you something," Relly said. Then Relly waved his grandfather to the apartment door.

"You better hope there's cake left when you get back," Bobby joked. The cake could wait.

Outside of the apartment, in the basement hallway,

Relly pressed the button for the elevator. Relly and Grandpa Gregory stepped on. Then Relly pressed the button for the roof. At the rooftop, the elevator opened to another hallway. At the end was a door. Relly pushed until it opened. A breeze of Harlem air spread around Relly and Grandpa Gregory. Relly led his grandfather to the middle of the roof. Grandpa Gregory took a glance around.

"Your father brought me up here when you were first born," Grandpa said, walking over to the empty pots. "Told me he was going to turn this place into a garden."

"He did," Relly said.

"That kid could tell me the name of anything that grew out the ground." Grandpa Gregory laughed. "Even the weeds! Oh, the memories. Lloyd used to be all over this city."

"Yeah, I know!" Relly laughed; then his tone got serious. "Grandpa, what would my dad think about me now?"

Grandpa Gregory did a slide. It was a simple left to right from the bench and pots to the middle of the rooftop.

"Grandson, I'm positive the two of you would be best friends."

Relly nodded. He pictured Lloyd with his satchel full of flyers. Lloyd's big eyes and his secret handshake.

"I'm going to bring it back."

"The garden?" Grandpa asked.

"The garden," Relly said. Then Relly reached for his

phone. On the verge of turning on his playlist, Relly began to listen. Around them was the sound of Harlem. Relly put his phone back in his pocket. For music, they had the city. They had the sound of shoes against pavement from down below. They had the sound of doors opening and doors closing. Babies crying and cars honking. Radios blasting and some late-night guitar player strumming. Trucks screeching and the distant murmur of a streetlight buzzing. The sound of a loose gutter banging against the side of Vanderzee Heights.

This was the beat of the city. This was the sound of Harlem. Relly began to tap to that beat. Shuffles and time steps and toe taps and riffs. Scissors and soft shoe and heel digs, too. Grandpa Gregory smiled ear to ear. He watched until he finally joined in with Relly. Underneath Harlem's sky, above Harlem's sidewalks, grandpa and grandson tapped. Then they slid together.

When Relly looked up, he knew one of those stars was his father, watching.

Jimmy Slyde

THE REAL SLYDE WAS BORN JAMES TITUS GODBOLT
on October 27, 1927. At twelve, the same age as Relly Morton,
James Titus Godbolt was a kid living in Boston, Massachusetts.
His mother wanted him to play the violin, but James had other
plans. His feet wanted to move, a feeling no violin could con-
tain. Lucky for James, the Stanley Brown Dance Studio across
the street from his violin lessons held the answers.

There, James was taught a sliding technique by a dancer
named Eddie "Schoolboy" Ford. This dance technique was
what James morphed into his unique signature trademark.
James transformed the taps on the bottom of his feet into a
smooth and delicate drawn-out rhythm. "The sound to me
is always important," he said in the book *Tap! The Greatest
Tap Dance Stars and Their Stories*. "Dancing is a translating
thing." James was influenced by jazz and picked up a keen
ear for sound. Soon, even his name slid into something new.

Slyde.

Slyde performed with the music of musicians such as
Duke Ellington and Count Basie. He encountered worry
over his career when rock and roll took over the musical
scene well into the nineteen fifties. But even through doubt,
worry, and fear, Slyde's career and his taps persevered. Over

time, he would become known as the King of Slide and the Godfather of Tap, a nickname coined by tap dancer Savion Glover.

Slyde passed away on May 16, 2008, but his legacy lives on. Numerous videos allow for us to continue to witness his tap-dancing prowess in the present day. Slyde performed around the world and went on to teach others his moves too. Dancing well into his seventies, Jimmy "Slyde" continued to be smooth on his feet, just as he had been at the age of twelve.

Acknowledgments

MANDY, I AM SO GRATEFUL THAT YOU ASKED ME to be part of book two. This book has been an adventure. It has been a cumulation of so many aspects in life that I love. Family, history, and theater. I am in awe over your confidence and your talent. You are mighty, and you are a force. You inspire me to push through each day with fearlessness. I appreciate your warmth, your kindness, honesty, and friendship. Thank you for looking out for little ole me, for meeting up in New York City and traversing midtown just like the Squad. Your ideas have sparked within me an investigation of my own talents, to be fearless in this vast world and to get out of my own comfort zone. I am so honored to be part of the #fearlesssquad.

To my incredible agent, Marietta Zacker, for first believing in me and for always believing in my words. Thank you for taking the time to listen, especially through the days when doubt left me wondering. I appreciate you for your honesty, understanding, and for always asking the hard questions. Your wisdom over these few years continues to make me a better author and collaborator. Most of all, a better me. I am beyond grateful for you.

To Alyson Heller, our brilliant editor. I am so appreciative of your time and willingness to meet via Zoom to answer my bounty of questions. I thank you for your editorial eye, your understanding, and all your support. Thank you to all those at Simon & Schuster.

To my friends Daria Peoples, Mike Jung, Victoria Coe, Robin Yardi, and Alicia D. Williams. I am grateful for your listening ear. Your writing advice has helped hone my craft through so many stories. I always value our time together. You are each an inspiration to me, and I could not ask for better friends.

To my former professors and friends at the Carnegie Mellon University School of Drama and Kingston University, London, Drama Department, you took my love of watching the stage and turned it into adoration for crafting stories and plays. For that I am thankful.

Finally, to my family. To my beautiful grandmother, Frances Juanita Thurman, who sparked the name for Nita's Bodega. You are my best friend, and I am so grateful to have a grandmother as wondrous as you. Thank you for listening to my laughs and my tears. Thank you for always saying there is nothing I cannot do. You, Gran-Gran, deserve the world, and I am so honored to be able to show the world to you. To my bold momma, Tia Thurman, who instilled in me a love for the stage when I first saw you perform Maya Angelou's "Still I Rise." You have sacrificed in ways I will never know. Through it all, you've taught me how to strive and to never be afraid to reach for my goals. I am blessed to call you my mother.

—Brittany

WRITING A STORY ABOUT THEATER DURING A Broadway shutdown that lasted eighteen months turned out to be a healing experience.

To think about all of the fearless performers who came before us, who overcame their own struggles that ultimately changed us all for the better left me hopeful. I believed to my core that Broadway would reopen, and that we would continue to tell our stories . . . together!

So much of that belief is also inspired by the collaboration with my Fearless Squad.

Brittany Thurman, working with you has been such a bright light during this time. Thank you for sharing your unending curiosity and enthusiasm. You are an incredible talent, and have become a great friend. Here's to our many future trips to Shubert Alley!

Thank you to our editor, Alyson Heller, for your guidance, and for always taking our Zoom calls with a smile. I am so thankful for you!

Cary Albertine and Saira Rao at All Together Media, thank you for always believing in these stories! You guys are the best!

ACKNOWLEDGMENTS

A big thank you to my agent, Jess Regel at Helm Literary, for your wisdom and guidance! You allow me to be fearless!

Ally Schuster, thank you for dreaming BIG!

Thank you to the team at Aladdin for lifting up and giving your support to this series.

Geraldine Rodriguez, you have done it again, hermana! Thank you for creating such an awesome cover!

I have to thank my first tap-dance teacher, John Zerby, who taught me to admire and respect the art form.

A big shout-out to all the librarians who have added the Fearless series to their reading lists. I appreciate all that you do!

Lou D'Ambrosio, thank you for always believing that anything and everything is possible.

Alexa D'Ambrosio, you are the best! Thank you for always answering all my calls, and for always saying with enthusiasm: "YES!"

Sending love to my mom, dad, Monica, Anthony, Ale, Audrey, and Gianna. It's been two years since I've been able to see you, and I miss you. I know we'll be together soon.

And my best friend, Darrell Moultrie. I love you so much!

To my husband, Douglas Melini, and our daughter, Maribelle. We have been through quite a ride these past two years, and we made it! Te quiero hasta la luna.

—Mandy